Rebel Bushwhacker

By

Wally Avett

W & B Publishers
USA

Rebel Bushwhacker © 2015. All rights reserved by Wally Avett

No part of this book may be reproduced or transmitted in any form or by any means, graphic, electronic, or mechanical, including photocopying, recording, taping, or by any informational storage retrieval system without prior permission in writing from the publisher.

W & B Publishers

For information:
W & B Publishers
Post Office Box 193
Colfax, NC 27235
www.a-argusbooks.com

ISBN: 9781942981-01-5
ISBN: 1942981-01-5

Book Cover designed by Dubya
Printed in the United States of America

ACKNOWLEDGEMENTS

This book is a fictional treatment based on real-life incidents from the War Between the States, in the immediate area where North Carolina, Georgia and Tennessee borders join.

The generous efforts of two local historians to inform the author on these matters is gratefully acknowledged.

The Madden Branch Massacre is key to this novel. It actually occurred a few miles downstream from the Ocoee Whitewater Center (originally constructed as the 1996 Atlanta Olympics whitewater venue.)

The late John B. Kimbrough lived near the site and provided invaluable oral history on the survivor and the victims.

The late Robert B. Barker of Andrews, N. C., for years did research on Civil War soldiers in Washington and produced a large volume of documents, now gathered in the McClung Collection at the Knox County Library in Knoxville, Tennessee.

In 2011 the State of Georgia erected a historical monument to the massacre. It is on the Ocoee River bridge at nearby McCaysville, naming both the young victims and the killer.

DEDICATION

This book is Civil War historical fiction, a storyteller's attempt to entertain and enlighten.

I hereby dedicate it to the Avett family – loud, boisterous, loving jokesters who hold annual reunions where we eat hearty, longingly remember, tell contrived narratives and play and sing gospel music.

Our grandfather, James Ira, oldest son of an ex-Confederate sergeant, passed from the scene early but I always absorbed the tales of the elders and soon learned the magic of stories.

These days our reunions often come in the form of funerals or weddings. But always with stories galore.

Lest we forget…

Chapter One

"Hurrah fer th' South! Hurrah fer the brave Tennesseans!" He shouted at the top of his lungs, nearly hoarse with excitement. "'Hurrah! Hurrah fer my brave Rebels!"

Spurring his horse down the wooden sidewalks of tiny Athens, Tennessee this fine Fall morning, the wild-eyed giant punctuated his shouting with random shots from the heavy revolvers in each hand.

"Victory!" he howled, firing a volley into a store window and sending the clerk and customers scurrying for safety. "Victory!"

The rag-tag gang of thieves and cutthroats who served him this morning numbered only ten, but they were following their leader and their animal instincts with merciless efficiency.

"It's Big Tobe Kirkwood," a civilian hissed in the mayor's ear.

"I'd recognize that red hair o' hisn anywheres."

A kindly Presbyterian who feared daily for his little town, the mayor temporarily lost control of his bladder at the mention of the dreaded Kirkwood Bushwhackers. The warm spreading stain on his trouser was embarrassing, but the thought of the Kirkwood gang in his town was just too much to bear.

The citizen saw his mayor's discomfort and thought nothing of it.

He plunged from the office into an alley beside the livery stable and the mayor turned over his chair in his haste to run, too.

In their private thoughts the mayor's momentary loss of dignity was instantly forgotten, blown away in the gun smoke and dust and noise of the bushwhacker gang's insistent presence in their very own town. Both men were panic-stricken, as was the whole town, hoping and fervently praying to survive, to live through the next five minutes. Living through the rest of the War Between the States would be another concern, a distant one at this point.

"Kill the sorry bastards," Kirkwood screeched, pointing a now-empty revolver across the street at two bewildered Union soldiers.

"Shoot the shit out of 'em! Gimme a damn rifle!"

Both cooks for a Federal encampment at nearby Loudon, the blue- uniformed men had ridden into a sleepy town to buy supplies and now found themselves in a hellish hornets' nest of flying bullets, cursing men, dust and sheer terror mixed in equal parts. Afoot and unarmed, they staggered from the store into the street and now stood paralyzed in fear and confusion.

The bearded bushwhackers bore down on them, some firing from the saddle, others jerking their horses to a halt and dismounting to shoot. They were firing rifles at short ranges and the two cooks fell kicking spasmodically in the dirt and manure of the street, each man hit at least a half-dozen times.

"Good enough for 'em," Kirkwood snarled, forcing his horse to walk back and forth over the bodies, trampling the Union corpses. The animal squealed and tried to sidestep the fallen men, but the smiling bushwhacker chieftain jerked it back to the grisly task and the animal's steel-shod hooves mangled the dead men again and again.

"By God, I git first look at th'r hosses," Joe Graddy said; Kirkwood's lieutenant, he was the only other man the bushwhackers would take orders from.

"I wanna see if they had any car'tr'ges fer this gun."

Graddy, the scout and sometimes the brains of the gang, was shooting a Spencer carbine they had liberated from a Union man over in North Carolina a month previous and it was almost out of shells. The factory-manufactured ammunition was impossible for the Southerners to duplicate; they could shoot the breech-loading rifles only as long as stolen ammunition lasted.

"Ain't a damn thing here I want," he said disgustedly moments later, ripping through the saddlebags of the Union men. "Nothin' but letters from home, Bibles, shit such as that."

He scattered the personal belongings of the two dead Union men in the street and another bushwhacker took control of the two federal mounts. Stripped of their US marked saddles, the two horses could be sold back to Union quartermasters in Knoxville for gold money.

Horses and mules were the main booty of the raid and the gang gathered them up in earnest now. Kirkwood swaggered through a deserted store but found little to amuse himself. Any store goods which were taken would have to be transported on horseback through the mountains and would only be a nuisance, especially if they were followed and it turned into a horse-race.

Graddy pawed through the drawers under the counter and the boxes on shelves behind the counter and found nothing of interest. They finally took one new frying pan and Kirkwood picked up a new hat for himself. Seizing a plume from a ladies hat, he stuck it into the headband of his new hat and proudly wore it out of the store, the feather waving at a jaunty angle.

"How 'bout that, Graddy? Don't I look like a cav'ry man now?"

"Yeah, Tobe, ya' look like Custer."

"Custer, my ass, I'll shoot hell out o' Custer if I ever see that Yankee sunofabitch."

"Yeah, I bet you will. L'es git, we got a bunch o' stock to move."

The gang gathered the horses and mules in the nearby main street, forty all told. They had found them tied along the street and had also gone into the barns and stables of the town itself, finding no opposition at all. Fearful owners had watched from behind curtained windows as the filthy marauders entered their barns and in many cases took family buggy horses which had been quietly munching hay only minutes before.

"It's Kirkwood for sure," one trembling merchant told his wife.

"They call him the red-headed beast; his trademark a pistol shot right in the face. That way he can't miss."

They watched in horror as Graddy and another raider dragged the mayor, begging pathetically and crying, from his hiding place in the livery stable and onto the street.

"Look who we found, Tobe, sez he's the mayor o' this place."

"See if he's got a watch on him."

The terrified man looked up at Kirkwood, mounted on his horse, and back down to the ground again and again, his head bobbing up and down. He made no protest as the two who held him prisoner went through his pants pockets. Graddy took the man's pocketknife for his own use and tossed the gold pocket-watch up to Kirkwood.

"Looks like a fine watch, you might really be the mayor."

Kirkwood casually leaned back over his saddle; he enjoyed holding court over his subjects. With his right hand, he lifted the flap on his saddlebag and deftly dropped the watch inside. Then his hand disappeared into the saddlebag for a moment and then reappeared, holding a fresh pistol, capped and loaded.

Smiling fiendishly, he stared into the doomed man's eyes and held his attention as a serpent might charm a helpless songbird. The mayor's eyes were locked in the cold stare of the bushwhacker as Kirkwood brought up the pistol and his grimy thumb pulled the hammer back to full cock with a series of metallic clicks.

He pressed the trigger and the piece fired, Kirkwood leaning forward from the saddle toward his target, closing the range to less than three feet. The pudgy mayor rose on his tiptoes at the impact of the lead ball in his face and then simply toppled over backward in a cloud of gun smoke .

Graddy and the others laughed, and one of them stole the mayor's boots. The man lay dead facing upward, his face blackened and powder-burned by the shot, a raw bloody hole just above the left eye.

Kirkwood gave the rebel yell, again and again, standing in his stirrups and waving the smoking pistol.

"Boys, they'll shore remember us now in Tennessee. Le's ride."

It had all happened in less than 30 minutes and they rode swiftly away into the Hiawassee River wilderness just south of the Great Smoky Mountains.

***

There were wild rivers here and high mountains, great tracts of virgin timber untouched by saw or axe. Giant poplars along the water-courses and tall brooding balsams and the stately American chestnuts which fed man and beast with their bounty in autumn.

For it was early Fall even now, the last day of September 1864, and a great war raged across the country. Here in the mountains where North Carolina and Tennessee and Georgia joined together, the war was different from the seaboard of Virginia where the great battles were fought. Here in the mountains it was a quiet, a personal struggle, often as intimate as a knife in the ribs or a shot from ambush. It was whispered rumors in the marketplace, which led to midnight raids by partisans of one side or the other. There were assassinations and kidnappings and revenge then taken, like an endless feud between two large families.

There was very little level land in the mountains which could lend itself to cotton growing, so there were very few slaves and no white-columned mansions. The landholders were largely Scotch-Irish, a fierce people dedicated to making children, whiskey and music, though not necessarily in that order. They also fought each other before the war over matters of honor or stolen property, and stoutly resisted all government.

***

When the war broke out, there were mixed feelings in the mountain strongholds. Confederate conscription officers were shot at and chased away as the struggle dragged on. There were strong pro-Union sentiments in many sections and an even stronger desire to be left alone, to fight for neither side.

And slavery, in a perverse indirect way, figured in this situation strongly. In the cotton-growing farmlands of the South, black slaves faithful to their owner-families could still grow some sort of field crops, pitiful though they might be, which would be enough to keep the white families alive.

In the mountains, however, the only labor available had always been free white labor. So families which gave their fathers or sons for Confederate soldiers had to have them back soon, to do the work and feed the home population.

Confederates deserted and came home to stay, to protect their families from pro-Union bushwhackers and to grow food for their own. Confederate Home Guard units in the towns often harassed Union families and did not dare to venture into rural sections where they were outnumbered by Unionists.

Deserters from both sides lay out in the woods and mountains, brutalized by the war, reduced to stealing and killing and a life of the outlaw. Law and order were gone forever, it seemed, and the country careened toward an unknown future.

***

"Reckon th' war's ever gonna end, Tobe?" Graddy asked, as they rode out of Athens.

"Hope not," Kirkwood grinned. "This is fun, ain't it?"

"Yeah, but if it ever ends, there'll be soldiers in here to stop us."

"Better shut up and ride.

"They'll have soldiers after us now for this."

They pushed the stolen horses and mules hard all day, fording the Hiawassee twice as they followed a faint trail in the wilderness. Late in the day they crossed over into North Carolina, although the state line meant nothing, and turned more to the south.

Their destination was a campsite they used rarely, on the high ground above the Nottley River near Murphy. The Home Guard at Murphy were infrequent allies and sometimes shared rations and conversation with the Kirkwood guerillas. The red-maned bushwhacker had strong Southern loyalties mixed with his wickedness. His followers, however, were mostly bandits and the Home Guard recognized them as such.

"Ya' gon' share these hosses with th' Murphy Home Guards?" Graddy asked.

"Might. Might sell some of' em, too."

They pushed on into the night, helped by a full moon and soon reached the campsite. Horses were quickly tied along a picket line and Graddy built a large fire.

"That big f'ar mite not be a good idea, Joe."

"Hell, Tobe, ain't nobody followin' us. 'Sides, I git cold."

Kirkwood shook his head. Early in the war he had been a sergeant in a regular uniformed Confederate outfit, fighting up in Virginia. But discipline among the guerillas was non-existent and sometimes it bothered him. No guards at night, nothing.

His men feared him personally, for his lethal skill with firearms and for his ferocious temper and his cunning plans. He killed often, with no remorse at all and no mercy, and they respected that. Beyond that, he commanded them with a careless manner which invited disaster. Vaguely, in the back of his mind, he knew it. He had assigned one man sentry duty once and the fellow had gone to sleep. It was hopeless.

"Speakin' o' f'ar, I like to see f'ar. Tobe, ya' ought to let us burn up a store er a house next time "

"Yeah, yeah, next time we hit a town, we'll leave a place burnin', so they'll remember us better."

He laughed and the bushwhackers howled with glee. By God, they'd burn down a fine painted house next time, they said.

Weary from the day's hard ride, they rolled into dirty black blankets and slept on the ground, there in the woods above the gurgling Nottley. The river turned and rolled over the worn boulders below, churning into ceaseless whitewater. The whip-or-wills called through the night and the yellow moon rose higher in a cloudless sky.

And from the top of the ridge across the river, hidden eyes watched Graddy's fire.

***

"Hey, Buck Rose, get ta' pullin' er' we'll never git done."

"Ol' man, y'er a slave-driver. Too bad we ain't got no niggers to do this job."

"Never could afford none, cost too much money."

"Well, I ain't one."

"But ya' don't mind a-sharin' in this corn, now do ya'?"

Buck Rose grinned at Old Man Tysinger and they went at it again pulling corn and joking each other in the hot sun.

"Now, 'day's the first, ain't it?"

"Yeah, first day o' October. We'll see frost f'er sure a-fore the month's out. Time's a-flyin'."

"How much longer this war gonna last?"

"Don't know, Buck, don't know. I'm an old man, family's all gone don't keer much what happens."

"Well, you hang aroun' down at th' Jail mor'n I do. Ya' hear the talk, what's the Guard sayin'?"

"Hell, they don't know nuthin'. Bunch o' old men like me an' real young boys. Hangin' on th' best they can, tha's all."

"Shore 'preciate ya' lettin' me come and pull some o' this corn f'er my family," Buck said. The younger of the two, he was doing most of the work, which was the plan they had agreed upon. The hard white corn would feed his saddle horse this coming winter and could also be ground into meal for his family.

Both men were Southern sympathizers, sometime members of the Confederate Home Guard. The Guard had taken over the Cherokee County jail in Murphy, beside the Courthouse, after executing the elected Sheriff, a Union man. In the absence of law and order, the Guard operated freely here in the westernmost tip of the North Carolina mountains. The jail was headquarters and served as a commissary for the Confederate cause. Food and materials were seized by force from Union families and kept at the jail, to be given to Confederate soldiers or Southern sympathizers as needed.

"They got a little corn down at the jail," Buck said. "But they keep it back fer th' Guard's hosses mostly. They're expectin' some o' Thomas's Legion in, too. In a week er so an' they'll need some."

Thomas's Highland Legion, one of the most colorful units in the Confederate Army, was recruited in the mountain country by the trusted chief of the Cherokees, a white man named Will Thomas. It was made up of both whites and Indians and their savage battlefield assaults, which began with Cherokee war cries and sometimes ended with dead and wounded enemies being scalped, made them instant legends in the Smokies.

"Thomas's Legion," the old man mused. "Never thought I'd see the day when white people would be fightin' on the same side as Indians."

"Oh, they're solid fer the Rebel side."

"Yeah, but it is sorta funny, now ain't it? Ch'rkees fightin' fer white people an' they got a white man fer th'r chief."

"He's a charmer, that Thomas is," Buck said, tossing another armload of corn into the cart between them. "I met him once right ther' in Murphy. He's got stores in ever' one o' th' towns 'roun here and he politicks the best I ever saw. No wonder he's chief of the Indians. They trust him. Lord, he could be anything he wants to."

The work and the talk ebbed and flowed between the two men, punctuated with trips to the corn-crib to empty the cart, the old man's horse plodding along and pulling the cart between them.

But Buck had been seen leaving Murphy to ride out to Old Man Tysinger's place that morning and the spy had checked on the corn pulling in mid-afternoon, just to make sure.

"Old Man Tysinger's got a purty good corn crop," he said that night, at a meeting of four Unionists in a cabin on Shoal Creek. "Buck Rose rode out from Murphy today to help'im pull it. They worked all day and I'd say they'll work all day tomorrow, too. The's enough of it it'll shore keep 'em busy fer a day 'er two."

The others nodded and grimly shook hands with the youth, not old enough to have a beard yet, who had brought them the news.

Buck Rose and Old Man Tysinger were minor members of the Murphy Home Guard. Not leaders, but sure-enough members of the outfit that had executed their Union-loyal sheriff and his sons over a year ago.

"That cornfield's shore a lonely place," one muttered. "Damn Jeff Davis trash."

***

The Union commander was a sturdy railroad man in civilian life, accustomed to bossing other men, but not used to riding horses through the mountains. Now, curiously, he found himself crouched in the darkness on foot, dripping wet from the knees down, taking orders from a civilian.

They had been called to Athens. Things happened so fast it seemed like years ago, but actually it was only about twenty-four hours or less. Yesterday morning, that's when it was, yesterday morning the bushwhackers had hit Athens and left three bodies in the street, getting away with a lot of horses and mules.

Two of the dead men were their cooks, good men, harmless and liked by all the men in the Ohio outfit. Now they were dead, shot down in the street by Rebel riff-raff. His men were mad, he was mad, and then, by sheer luck, they were approached by a civilian who offered to serve them as a scout.

The man had been a cattle-buyer before the war and knew the mountains well, on both sides of the Tennessee-North Carolina border. He knew animals and he could track. His uncle was the dead mayor, found lying in the street after the raid.

"It's Big Tobe Kirkwood and his bushwhackers," he told the Union captain. "Several people saw him, there's no mistaking that red hair and beard o' his. Confederate guerilla, mean as holy hell."

"What was he doing in Athens?"

"Stealing horses, mostly. Usually stays south of here. He's a bad 'un, but ya' got him outnumbered, f'er sure. Best I can tell, he's got less than a dozen men with him this time."

"Draw rations for every man for two days only," the Union captain snapped out his orders. "Be ready to ride in a quarter-hour."

***

With the scout leading them, the eighty Ohio men had ridden a hard trail all day. They had forded rivers and pushed on through virgin stands of dark timber, following the bushwhackers and their stolen stock.

"He's headin' south, hard as they can go, fer Murphy," the scout said. "From what they say, Kirkwood works sometime with the Home Guard down there. Maybe they wanted the horses, maybe he'll sell 'em."

As the day drew near to a close, the scout cautiously probed ahead alone, bringing up the Union troops with hand motions. The full moon enabled them to travel on easily and the scout finally stopped them.

"Don't camp," he instructed their captain. "Just let them rest their horses. Don't build any fires and don't go to sleep. I'll ride on alone for a while and come back shortly. If they hear our horses just one time, they'll be on the alert."

"I'll send a man or two with you."

"No, I don't need any help."

"You may get ambushed, mister, they might jump you."

"Naw, they're tired, too. Lemme see if I can find their camp."

The weary soldiers dismounted and tied their horses and the scout rode off alone in the soft moonlight. He was near the Nottley River, he knew that from a cattle-buying trip into this country before the War. There was a ford somewhere up ahead and he sensed that the bushwhackers had crossed the river, perhaps gone all the way into Murphy, just a few miles ahead.

On top of the last ridge paralleling the river, he paused and looked across the mountain vista, bathed in moonlight. Distant peaks and ridges were lit almost bright as daylight.

As he sat on his horse and watched, he saw the flicker of Graddy's fire begin to build stronger and stronger on the next ridge beyond the river.

The scout smiled and turned his horse back toward the waiting Union troopers. It was around midnight according to his pocket watch, there was plenty of time to do what had to be done.

***

"They're camped just across the river, on top of a wooded ridge, about two miles from here," he told the captain and the sergeants. "We'll ride in a little closer, then leave the horses before we get close enough for their horses to smell ours and start a racket. Go in on foot, ford the river and be waiting in the timber, right on top of 'em, when daylight comes."

It was decided, since the enemy was so close and the ground could be covered quickly, to allow the men one hour's sleep. This was received gratefully and the men literally slept where they fell, worn out from the day's ride, their horses tied and saddled near them.

The officers did not sleep, and within the allotted time, woke the men and the whole outfit mounted up, to follow the scout for about a mile on the trail. Then the horses were tied to trees and two men were left with them. The rest proceeded on foot, roughly grouped in four squads, following the scout.

Down to the ford they walked, as quietly as possible. The moon was low now and the light not as good as earlier in the night. The river water was cold and a good current washed their legs as they all floundered across, getting wet to the knees. The river was noisy with whitewater anyway, constant rushing and gurgling being a part of normal sounds, so the sloshing of nearly eighty men crossing it was not noticed. Up the hill they trudged, wet and miserable now, led by the whispering, hissing scout.

"Hey! Hey! Careful! Easy now, hush that cussin'."

Like the drifting cloud-fog that moves silently into the coves and hollows, the Union men simply appeared here and there in the campsite. Moving quietly, they eased in among the horses, toward the sleeping figures around the glowing campfire.

Birds were chirping now in the first light of morning and the federals were inside the camp on three sides when one of the Ohio farm boys, his thumb on the hammer of his pistol, tripped over a tree-root and fell forward. Accidentally, his thumb ripped the hammer backward and let it go as he fell. The pistol fired, the slug plowing into the upper thigh of the man in front of him and the element of surprise was suddenly lost.

The man who was shot screamed loudly and that,

along with the pistol shot, awakened the sleeping bushwhacker camp.

In a split-second it seemed that all hell broke loose.

The rebels rolled out of their dirty blankets, reaching for hidden guns, firing blindly in all directions and running, running away from the blazing guns of the Union soldiers.

"Shoot 'em down, men. Aim low. Don't let 'em get away," the federal captain ordered. His voice was strong, but not excited, as if giving directions for splitting wood or some other such camp chore.

Bullets whined through the trees like angry hornets and horses bawled in terror when struck by stray lead. Two of the bushwhackers were downed immediately and the federals continued to shoot into their bodies for several seconds as the men twitched on the ground.

"Hurry! They're getting away," the captain said. Following his advice, the federals began to deliberately shoot low, hitting the guerillas in the legs and then finishing them off one by one as they staggered and fell.

The scout had actually entered the ring of sleeping men just before the accidental pistol-shot woke them and paid dearly for his bravery. Instead of shooting , the scout was looking frantically for the tell-tale red hair of the legendary Kirkwood.

Obsessed with finding the bushwhacker chief, he was shot and killed on the spot by Graddy, who awoke to find upright figures walking in the camp and began firing by instinct. His pistol bucked and roared and two more Union men fell wounded.

Graddy ran toward the horses, but was felled by a mini-ball in the leg and then shot twice more through the body by the Ohio men and died kicking in the leaves, staring upward at the dawn sky.

Big Tobe Kirkwood usually slept in his filthy drawers, rolled up in a blanket. At the sound of the first shots, he clawed his way out of the blanket and ran like a deer. His large white body made a good target as he dodged through the trees, but the Union marksmanship was poor in the dim light of dawn and though bullets clipped bark around him, at first none hit him.

Kirkwood was unarmed and only his dirty shorts covered his nakedness. He ducked and darted and was nearly to the horses when the first lead slug tore his flesh. It struck him a glancing lick just above the knee, tearing the outer muscle of the thigh; the impact of which caused him to fall momentarily.

"He's down, boys, pour it on," a Yankee sergeant swore. "The damn bastard's gonna get away clean."

Bullets kicked up forest dirt and leaves around him, but somehow missed the red-headed guerilla, who got to his feet and ran on. It was only ten yards now to the nearest horses tied in the trees.

Kirkwood reached the horses, untied one and managed to mount, but just as he had the animal free and ready to go, two bullets hit him in the upper body and he toppled over, falling from the horse's back heavily to the ground.

With a superhuman effort, Kirkwood groaned and dragged himself to his feet, facing his enemies.

The nearest Ohio man, skilled in squirrel-hunting before the War and handy with a rifle, leveled his piece and drew aim on the nodding head of the bleeding bushwhacker. He pulled the trigger, sure of his target.

The heavy .50-calibre mini-ball struck the side of

Kirkwood's head, severing the upper half of the ear in the process, and for the guerilla leader, who felt himself falling toward the ground, all was suddenly blackness.

Chapter Two

Buck Rose and Old Man Tysinger were nearly done with the corn harvest. Although it had a lot of weeds in it, the older man had produced a good crop and was glad to have Buck come out from Murphy and help him pull it, slowly filling the log corn-crib beside his ramshackle barn.

"A little cornbread'll eat good this winter, won't it, Buck?"

"Yeah, an' the hosses'll eat good, too."

They tossed the ears of corn, in pale white shuck, into the little one-horse cart of the old man. His horse patiently pulled the load up and down the rows until they had it filled. Then they would rest a few minutes and take the cart to the crib to empty it.

The war and the fighting seemed a million miles away, they had not seen or heard a soul all day. The old farm was in a remote section and, aside from the normal sounds of birds and insects, it was peaceful and quiet... very quiet.

The Union men from Shoal Creek were also very quiet in their work.

Led by the young boy, who was visibly nervous over this mission, they tied their horses a half-mile away in the woods and crept into the farm in mid-afternoon. Rutted tracks left by the cart and broken-down weeds near the crib told the story, plain as day.

"Wait fer 'em here," the bearded leader grunted. "They'll be back by-n-bye, ain't goin' nowheres." The men and the boy hid and waited in the barn, watching the trail from the cornfield.

They were not disappointed.

In less than thirty minutes they heard the groaning and creaking of the loaded cart approaching, along with the voices of Buck Rose and Old Man Tysinger. They jumped the pair as they passed on the trail between the barn and the crib.

"Stand fast there, Buck, er I'll put a musket-ball th'u y'er gizzard," the bearded leader said. "Old man, stop the horse and drop the reins."

The two Home Guard men were shocked and surrounded before they could comprehend what was happening. The grinning Unionists were armed with rifles, one had a shotgun, all aimed at them.

"I know you," Buck said, glaring at the leader. "Y're from Shoal Creek. Lincoln-lovin' rogues, I hope ya' roast in hell, ever' one o' you."

"Anybody's gonna be in hell, it'll be you'uns, long before us," the other grinned. "We gonna see to that r'at now."

"Ain't no use in you'uns unloading that corn, we gon' take it an' the cart, too, when we're done," another said.

Ropes quickly bound the two men's wrists and they were taken to the barn, one of the Union raiders driving the cartload of corn along behind them.

"Keep ya' guns on 'em, boys, but the's one thang I gotta do a-fore we hang 'em," the leader said. He put his own rifle down and searched around in the barn until he found a clawhammer.

"This'll do fine," he said, walking up to the bound men. "You Home Guard sonsabitches shot our Shur'f over a year ago. Fer nuthin' 'cept he was a Union man. By God, fer nuthin'."

Seizing the old man by the throat with his left hand, the Union leader swung the hammer in a short vicious arc, clubbing Old Man Tysinger's head twice with measured blows. The victim groaned, but stayed on his feet, hot blood trickling down the side of his face and dripping off his chin.

"I ain't gonna kill you'uns with this hammer, we'll let the rope do that, but, by God, I want you'uns to feel some pain before you go. Here, Buck, this is fer you."

He whipped Buck around the head and shoulders with several more blows of the bloody hammer, the younger victim dodging some of the licks by shifting his weight on his feet under the attack.

"Stand still, damn you."

"Y'er a real brave fighter, Shoal Creek, hitting a man with a hammer when he's tied up."

"You ain't seen nuthin' yet," the leader said. "Back that cart in under that beam yonder. We gon' tie some more rope on you'uns, this time around y'er necks. Time fer a little dancin', ain't it, boys?"

With some rude laughter, the Unionists got the loaded cart in place and lifted their bound and bloodied enemies into standing positions on the mounded load of loose corn.

"Get some plow-lines, I seen some there in the shed," the leader said. "Don't mess with the harness on this cart-horse here. We'll take him and the cart and the corn too, when we finish this little job."

Rope was found, nooses were tied and the two

men were soon standing wobbly-legged on the pile of corn, looking up as their ropes were tied securely to a main beam in the barn-loft above them.

"Rebel trash, you'uns'll be in hell in five seconds," the leader promised. "Shur'f Gentry was a good man, by God, y'all deserve this."

No quarter was asked, none was expected. The leader nodded and one of the Shoal Creek men hit the cart-horse with a stick. The animal lunged forward and the two helpless men on the pile of corn toppled backward off the cart into eternity.

***

On the ridge-top above the Nottley River, all was quiet. With the last of the Kirkwood Bushwhackers down, the guns were silent.

"That's him, Captain, see that red hair?"

The federal officer and two of his sergeants were looking down at the sprawled figure of Big Tobe Kirkwood, bleeding from several wounds to the body, the head a solid mass of blood, half an ear missing.

"Dead as hell, sir, shot to pieces. Maybe we ought to cut the head off and take it back to Athens to show the people."

The captain grimaced in disgust and shook his head.

"No, we're not savages. They can take our word for it that he's really dead. They'll be more interested in getting their horses and mules back.

"And speaking of mutilating the dead, cutting heads off and such I don't plan to waste any time in leaving here. We're over into North Carolina, I know that. Can't be far from Murphy. Thomas's Legion ride these parts and they are known for taking scalps, from the wounded as well as the dead."

"Yeah, I heard about that," the sergeant said. "Some of them Indiana fellers they killed in the Baptist Gap fight had to get took home and buried without their hair."

"We left a good trail getting in here and we may have been seen, may have to fight our way back to Tennessee," the captain said. "How many casualties we got?"

After some checking, it was determined that the only death had been the civilian scout shot by Graddy. Five other men had been wounded, but all could ride, and were anxious to be leaving.

"Our scout's dead," the captain said. "He was a brave man, let's take him home to his family, if we can find our way back by ourselves." Noise of the battle had been heard in the early morning for some distance and curious residents found the site soon after the Union departure.

A ten-year-old boy was mounted on an aging plow-horse and sent galloping toward Murphy, to take the word to the Home Guard. The word-of-mouth grapevine spread the message throughout the little town in minutes, the message that Big Tobe Kirkwood and all his men lay dead on the Nottley.

***

"I hate diggin' these taters. I'druther go a-fishin'."

"I'm sure you would, little brother," Hattie June said. "Maybe we get done early, you can still go fishing."

They had a large garden, surrounded by a split-rail fence to keep free-ranging stock out of the vegetables. There was an old log cabin, a barn and some small outbuildings, along with some peach trees, long favored by both whites and Indians here in the mountains.

"Them Indians that built this place shore fixed it up nice, didn't they, Sis?"

She nodded, eyes on the rugged horizon, thoughts a thousand miles away. Their place had been the property of a Cherokee, long since removed to the West in what the Indians called the Trail of Tears. It had, of course, been appraised and paid for by white government men who summed up generations of native civilization with their words and numbers:

1 cabin $30, 1 Stable $15, Shed $5, 12 acres good river low ground @ $10, 3 acres cleared uncultivated upland @ $4, 30 acres fenced woodland@ $2, 35 peach trees@ .75, 2 apple trees@ $1 -- these Improvements Claimed by Hogshooter -- six in his family -- driven off land by whites

Hattie June knew well the history of their place, she could read as well as anyone in Murphy, just down the Hiawassee River a few miles. She had read the writings of the surveyors and appraisers who had measured the country before the Indians were removed, down at the Courthouse.

Actually, it was not a real courthouse, she knew that, it was just a large barracks building left over by the soldiers who had come here to take the Indians away. But for Murphy and Cherokee County, it now served as a good courthouse. The records were kept there and once in a great while they even had court there.

They had had a school, too, down in Murphy and she went there with enthusiasm for years. Other kids might gripe about books and numbers and such, but Hattie June loved it. She read everything she could get her hands on and it took her into a secret world beyond these rugged wooded mountains. She had read of cities and ships and railroads and she was anxious to see the world outside, sometime.

"At least I don't hafta go to school," her younger brother giggled, raking out another handful of potatoes from the soft bottom- land soil. "I hope the War goes on for a long time."

"You hush," she scolded. "The War's gonna end and you'll be back in school soon enough."

The War had taken their school and changed life in other ways. Hattie June was 18, six years older than her brother, and would probably have been married by now if things were normal. She thought about marriage often and found herself looking at some of the uniformed Confederates who came through periodically with strange feelings.

In her heart, she wanted to marry a stranger and live in a big city, where there were street-cars and lights and music and fancy doings.

Granny, who was in the cabin fixing their supper, pushed her toward this possible suitor or that, but it was all talk.

"Set y'er cap f'er that Higgins boy, he's home on furlough. I heered it on market day."

Market day was Saturday in the little country towns like Murphy, regardless of the War. Folks from out in the county came into town to do their business and their trading and what little buying they could do, and to gossip and talk and exchange rumors and news.

But the Higgins boy, and others like him, did not interest her. Hattie June wanted it to end and hoped that she might be a schoolteacher. She had been helping teach the little ones when the school finally petered out three years ago and she had not forgotten anything, she was sure of that. When things went back to normal, she could be a teacher and get paid for it.

"I hear somebody ridin' up the river, don't you?"

Her brother's question jarred her back to reality. In the stillness, they could plainly hear a horse's hooves drumming on the rocky wagon road which paralleled the Hiawassee from Murphy to Brasstown.

"Maybe it's Papa."

"No, too early for him."

The hooves grew louder and it became apparent that the rider was not going to proceed on to Brasstown, but was coming into their little farm.

The rider appeared. It was an old man from Murphy they both knew well, a member of the Home Guard. He rode up to the garden fence and sat still on his horse for a moment, looking down at them.

He took his hat off, shook his head gravely and spoke to them.

"I got some bad news, some mighty bad news for you, Hattie June Rose. An' for you too, Little Buck."

***

Fearful of facing the mixed Indian and white troops of Thomas's Legion and thereby losing their hair, the Ohio unit left quickly with the dead and wounded, gathering up the stolen horses and mules and riding toward Athens.

The bushwhackers lay where they had fallen, some with their weapons still beside them. Their horses were taken by the federals, so no animals greeted the first arrivals on the site.

"Yah, Mama, here's one."

She did not speak, only grunting in agreement, as the old couple walked slowly over the battleground. Their cabin was only a mile away, they had heard the shooting plainly early this morning and had been frightened. Now, about noon, they had found the place and were very cautiously picking their way through it.

"Here's another, Mama, all dead."

There were ragged piles of blankets around a still-smoldering fire and through the trees, here and there, lumps of dark and twisted clothing. These turned out to be bearded men, dirty and bloody and very dead. Some still held weapons in their hands, pistols mostly. They found loaded rifles lying in the leaves next to some of the blankets where they had been sleeping. One dead horse also lay in the trees and the blue-green blowflies were beginning to swarm on the animal and soon would find the men.

At the edge of the site, they found the big man in his drawers. His size, and the fact that he had almost no clothes on, drew their attention.

"That one didn't have time to put his pants on, Mama."

They stood there looking down at bloody Tobe Kirkwood, hit in both legs and the upper body and the head. And he groaned slightly.

"Listen, Mama, that one is still alive."

She knelt down and cradled the red-haired head in her hands, brushing away the leaves and looking closely at the head wound. He groaned again, louder this time.

"Papa, maybe we can save this man. We ought to, if we can." The old man hurried back to the cabin, leaving her with the wounded man. They had an old plow-horse which he hitched to a sled and with some difficulty got it back through the timber to the battleground. He and the old woman then rolled the hurt man onto a blanket and half-carried, half-dragged the heavy body to the sled.

Kirkwood groaned frequently during the bumpy ride on the sled back to their cabin, but never regained consciousness. The old woman bathed him with tender hands, cleaning away the blood and dirt, and bound his wounds with strips of rags, stopping the bleeding. He lay on their bed and they slept on the floor that night, listening to his shallow breathing.

***

Late in the day, the Home Guard had sent men in and they were puzzled. They carried shovels and were soon busy burying the dead bushwhackers and gathering up the guns and blankets and anything else which could be used in the war effort.

"Whar's Kirkwood?"

"Hell, I don't know. Maybe a b'ar dragged 'im off."

"Naw, a b'ar mite eat a body after it's been dead a few days an' starts smellin', but not a fresh kill."

"Th' first people here wuz the Livengoods, the way I got it, and they plainly seen Kirkwood layin' dead. Sent the little boy to tell us. Now whur's Kirkwood?"

The burial party finished its work smartly, hurrying to beat darkness, and rode back to Murphy in the moonlight. Several expressed their desire not to spend the night on the battleground, in the presence of dead men, even if they had been casual acquaintances.

"Wuz Kirkwood ever in the r'agular army?"

"Yeah, I heered 'im tellin' some of 'em at the jail one day 'bout it. He started out as a sergeant in the infantry, fit the damn Yankees up in Virginny and got tired and come home. They call him a bushwhacker and I reckon he killed and robbed a lot, but by God, he done it f'er the Southern side."

"Maybe them Yankee soldiers come back and took him with 'em."

"Could have."

***

In the old couple's cabin, Kirkwood groaned and tossed on their bed, writhing in pain.

"He'll go into a fever," the old woman said confidently. Treating the sick was her skill and she enjoyed holding forth, even to an audience of only one. "His body is a-fightin' now, fightin' agin all these wounds and hit'll shore cause a fever. If the fever don't kill 'im, we mite stand a chance."

Nodding solemnly at her orders, the old man fetched buckets of water from their cold-running spring. She bathed the big red-head with rags dipped in the cool water for the rest of the night and all day.

His body trembled and the old man wondered whether it was from the fever or from having his limbs washed continually with the frigid mountain-spring water. The old woman bathed his head too, saturating the long red hair and the bearded face with ice-cold water. His body fought hard, the big chest heaving with deep breaths. He moaned with each breath, a low sound that came through gritted teeth and filled the little cabin with the sounds of his pain.

"He's young and he's strong, real strong," she said. "Go git some more water, the fever's weakening, I b'leeve we've got it whupped."

At the end of the day, some thirty-six hours after

he'd been shot by the Ohio troops, Kirkwood opened his eyes and stared strangely at his two keepers.

"Where... am...I?"

"Why, y'er here with us, in our cabin."

"What happened to the Yankees? Where's my men?"

"Yankees left, took all the horses. All y'er men are dead." Exhausted, he fell back on the pillow and stared upward, eyes blinking in slow comprehension. The fever was breaking and he did not resist as the old woman slowly washed him one last time with the cold spring-water. Before she finished, he was asleep in a deep, deep trance that seemed like death. His body was cool to the touch now and they all got a good night's sleep.

"My head hurts like the very devil," he told them the next morning. "I'm sore all over, but my head is killin' me."

"If ya' kin complain, it's a good sign," the old woman grinned. "No wonder ya' head hurts, they shot off half y'er ear and I guess the rifle ball musta bounced off y'er thick skull."

Kirkwood gingerly reached up and touched the side of his head, drawing back quickly when his probing fingers found the dried blood and mangled ear. Looking down over his body he winced when he saw the rags wrapped around his leg wounds and winced again as pain shot through him from the shoulder wound.

"I'm shot up purty good, ain't I?"

"Yeah, they shore meant f'er ya' t' die. The fever 'bout got it done yestiddy, but today ya' got a good chance. Got to work on them bullet holes now."

The old couple had a tar-kiln, a primitive arrangement made of stone that enabled them to cook pine wood and catch the rich resins that oozed from it. This sticky substance was used as a crude medicine for animals, and sometimes humans.

"Y'er lucky none o'them bullets hit a bone and they all went clean though," she said. "We gonna put some warm tar on them holes, let that good pine-sap pull the soreness out and scab over real good. When the scabs come off, y'll have a few scars, but y'll be good as new."

***

Hattie June Rose cried like her heart would break. At first she thought maybe it would, and she would die herself there in the garden, standing by the rail fence. Little Buck came to her, bawling like a baby, and she hugged him tight.

"We'll bring in the body, Hattie June," the patient Home Guard who had brought the dreadful message said to her, still sitting on his horse, touched by the scene unfolding in front of him.

"Some o' the folks down there think they seen the Bradfords comin' through, from off Shoal Creek. They think they probably done it."

She nodded in gratitude for this information. The Bradfords were a rough Union clan from the western end of the county, hard up against the Tennessee line. Now they had killed her father, hanged him and Old Man Tysinger, they said, in Old Man Tysinger's barn. Well, they would pay. They would all pay and pay in blood, she meant it.

Granny came out of the house at the commotion and received the news stone-faced, hugging her grandchildren and rocking slowly back and forth on her feet, holding them like they were babies again. Her only daughter, mother of these poor children, had died with the milk fever ten years ago and she had come to live with them and raise them up right. The girl had been eight then, the boy they called Little Buck only about two years old.

Buck Rose, her sturdy son-in-law, had been a good man, working at variety of jobs to keep the family together, mostly as a laborer on farms around Murphy. He could carpenter too, and had worked on building houses and barns, even a store or two. Now he was gone, hanged by Yankee bushwhackers from the lower end of the county. It was a cruel war that took men from their families.

"Some of our men are fixing a box to put'im in," the Home Guard said. "We'll bring 'im to you'uns this afternoon, have the funeral tomorrow in Murphy, if that suits. The way we see it, they musta jumped both of 'em and hanged 'em both late yesterday afternoon. We found 'em just this morning."

"Buck never come in last night," Granny said, "but we never thought nuthin' of it. He wuz out there helpin' Tysinger gither his corn, f'er a share of it he wuz gonna give Buck, and he'd been ridin' out there ever' day and comin' back here ever' night. We just figgered he decided to stay over one night at Tysinger's. We never knowed he 'uz dead."

The Home Guard brought Buck Rose's body to his house that very afternoon, a grim procession that included his horse, with the body wrapped in a blanket draped over the saddle, several of the Guard, and a wagon with a freshly-made coffin bringing up the rear.

"Y'all git Buck ready and we'll be back tomorrow to take him to town," the Guard captain said. "We got an ol' Methodist preacher that can say the funeral."

They had buried Buck Rose on the highest point in Murphy, the Methodist cemetery that overlooked the little town, right next to some of the Meroney graves. There was the preacher and some of the Home Guard, they even brought a Confederate flag. Hattie and Little Buck choked back the tears then and took it all in, the simple ritual of their father being laid to rest under a giant hemlock.

"The Lord is my Shepherd..." the old preacher droned on and she found little comfort in his holy words. Her eyes riveted on the blood-red Rebel flag and, in her mind, she swore vengeance on the awful Shoal Creek Union-loving trash that had hanged Buck Rose.

I'll be a sword of the Lord, like it says in the Bible, she promised herself and was surprised at her own deadly calm and fierce concentration. *Somehow I can find out who did it and help the Guard to get every one of them, I swear it on your grave here today, Papa. Blood and fire and destruction, I'll bring it down on their heads, Papa. Lord, give me the strength to get them.*

Seized with a cold fury, she was clenching her small fists together again and again, trembling all over, as the outdoor service ended. Her mind was focused, her future path was clear to her, how she would do it would have to be worked out, but she was going to be utter hell on Yankees around here from now on.

"That pore l'il Rose girl was shore takin' it hard," the Guard captain observed as the burial delegation rode back to their headquarters at the jail. "I went up to her at the end and tried to give a little hug to the pore thang, she wuz just a-shakin' all over."

***

In the next few days the Guard sent men down to Tysinger's place and they brought the Rose kids their father's half of the corn left in the crib, enough to feed the horse through the winter and have some meal ground for them to eat, too.

Granny bustled around, bossing Hattie and Little Buck into digging the rest of the potatoes and generally they got ready for cold weather and, once in a while, managed to forget for a few moments their terrible loss.

Two weeks later, on a Saturday, they all three went to Murphy to trade some eggs and try to find Granny some honey.

"Young'uns, these hens are layin' good right now and we'll make us a good trade, I just know it. Fresh cornbread goes good with honey on it, gotta get some honey."

Like other country people, they arrived in Murphy early, having hitched Papa's horse to the buggy soon after daylight. Four dozen eggs rode safely in the back in a basket guarded by Little Buck. They walked the streets, peered into the back of other folks' wagons at their wares, heard lots of sympathy for their tragic loss.

"Sorry t'hear 'bout Buck, it shore wuz a bad thang."

They nodded and made conversation about the weather and the War, showing their eggs, looking for some honey.

"Lemme see them eggs, girl," one of Granny's old-woman friends said. "Yeah, they look all right. Find some o' the Hyatts if ya' kin, they all keep bees and they'll have honey. Probably th'only ones here with honey t' trade."

Walking in the thick dust of the main street, they found the Hyatt wagons and Granny soon clutched a stone crock of pale clear honey while Little Buck swung a now-empty basket on his arm. A lone rider came slowly up the middle of the street and the market activity suddenly ceased and every head turned.

Hattie looked, too, at the strange man on the horse. He was big, dressed in rags, and the horse seemed to be an old gray plow-nag, so thin its ribs showed. It stumbled twice, but continued to carry the man up the street. On both sides of her, she saw hands raised and fingers pointing at the man and heard the low whispering begin, like the humming of summer flies.

"'At's Big Tobe Kirkwood, shore t'God it is," one of Granny's old-woman friends said. "The Unions shot 'im all to pieces two weeks ago over on the Nottley River, said they killed all his men and like to have kilt Tobe, too."

The old woman spat and continued. "I heered some oldtimers over th'ar nursed him up and there he is, so I guess it's so. Tobe's killed a lot of Yankees and I'd say it's gonna be pure old hell to pay roun' here now, he'll get 'im some more men and turn it loose on 'em."

Hattie stared in fascination now, entranced by the rawboned man on the horse. His head was bandaged with a rag, but the sun picked up the sheen of the carrot-red hair. Despite the wounds, he sat the nag proudly and stared coldly at the market crowd. The aging mount plodded up the street and turned into an alley, heading for the jail.

"He won't hurt y'all, or any o' us neither," the old woman told Granny, "but if ya' know any of these Union families, ya' kin tell 'im goodbye, 'cause it'll shore be rough on 'em now. Tobe Kirkwood is a bushwhacker fer the South and now he's gonna be meaner'n ever."

Chapter Three

"I hate 'em, Granny, I hate 'em ever' one."

"Who, child, who ya' talkin' about?"

"The Yankee-loving snakes, they're all around us. The ones who hanged our Papa, that's who. They killed Papa just like a dog and now they're laughing, I just know it."

"Hush, girl, just calm down," she murmured, patting her agitated granddaughter on the shoulder. They were peeling potatoes, some of the new crop, standing side-by-side.

"That man we saw at the market today, Granny, he looked like a tough one. I bet he's killed a lot o' Yankees."

"Ah yeah, Tobe Kirkwood, he's a bad 'un all right, but he's a bushwhacker, does about as much robbin' as he does fightin' fer the South. Robbed a few Rebs, too, they tell me, when it suits him, if they got anythang he wants."

"But he's brave, ain't he?"

"Oh shore, brave as a game rooster. I talked some to ol' Molly at the market this mornin' while you wuz walkin' around. She'd talked to them old folks that nursed him up out there on the Nottley. Said he tol 'em about it. Him and his men had killed three or four dozen Yankees at Athens, Tennessee, by Ned, and took all their horses, musta had a hundred er more. Wuz comin' back with 'em when they got jumped in th'r camp and ever' one killed 'cept Tobe, and him *almost* killed."

The very next Saturday they went back to Murphy, as was their custom, to trade and talk and Hattie heard more about Big Tobe Kirkwood. Fit as a fiddle, they said, except for a few scabs showing and they'll be falling off any day now. Mean as a snake and already a-gathering men for more Rebel mischief.

Home Guard had give him a good horse and some guns, the talk was, and he was camped somewhere back in on Wildcat Mountain, about a mile from town.

Walking through the market activity, Hattie stared sometimes at people she suspected of Yankee sympathy. Some of these talking and trading, looking at chickens for sale or honey or chestnuts or eggs or whatever, dickering over a trade and nodding and whispering, some of these may know who killed Buck Rose, in fact, may have been the very ones who sent word to Shoal Creek and set up the ambush. Oh, she hated these Yankee dogs, she began to tremble slightly and could not control herself.

An idea began to form itself in her head and at first she was afraid of it, but as she looked at it in her mind and gradually began to accept it, it seemed better. Surprised by her own boldness, she was soon proud of her new idea.

I want Granny to know, to know what I will do, and maybe to say it's all right. She's all I got now, she can look after Little Buck.

While her little brother was taking the harness off their horse and putting the buggy away, before she lost her courage, she went into the house with Granny and spoke bluntly.

"Granny, I've thought it over in my mind and I'm gonna leave. I'm going to the woods to join up with Tobe Kirkwood."

The old woman turned and faced her fully. She was surprised and a little bit frightened by the fierce stare in Hattie's eyes.

"Girl, that ain't smart. Women don't fight like men do."

"I don't care, I'm going anyway. Maybe I can't fight like a man, but I can think and talk and plan. I can go to market and talk to folks and find out things, spy for Kirkwood, help him find Yankees. I hate the ones that killed Papa, I want all the Yankees to die, Granny."

"Kirkwood ain't a saint, girl. He needs fightin' men, not a slip of a girl. He'll use ya' like a camp whore and then give ya' to his men t' use. Ye'll come back to us in a few months fat and swole up with a child."

She was speechless, she had not counted on that, she only wanted revenge, awful bloody vengeance, it had captured her mind.

"Granny, I'll be going," she said after a moment or two. "I'm going anyway. Help me get my things together in a sack. I'm taking Papa's horse and pistol." The old woman shook her head, but said no more.

She hugged Little Buck, who did not understand either, and rode away in a few minutes. There was some food in a sack, some clothing in another. After all, she would be in the same county, she told them, and could return from time to time to get anything she needed.

Papa's cap-and-ball revolver was in one saddle bag, a small butcher-knife went into the other one. Her father had shown them how to load and shoot the handgun many times before he died; Granny had shown her how to sharpen and use a knife, and how to butcher animals with it.

***

It was Saturday, mid-afternoon, when Hattie June Rose re-entered Murphy. This time she was riding a horse, alone, and what was left of the market crowd looked at her with curiosity, but nothing more. All sorts of strange things were happening now and Buck Rose's girl riding through town was not really that strange.

"She's not ridin' side-saddle, like a proper lady," one old crone remarked. "She's straddlin' that hoss jus' like a man, ain't that right?"

Her companion nodded and began anew the haggling process between them, over a short length of calico cloth. The Rose girl's riding posture was of little interest to anyone there.

Hattie turned the horse down toward the river ford and gently put the animal into the shallow water of the Hiawassee River, which split the town. The strong gelding waded through the boulders and mud quickly and gained the far bank, water streaming down his legs as he came up from the river onto the well-beaten wagon trail west.

Wildcat Mountain soon loomed high on her left, a rugged humpback that was now pretty with the colors of early autumn. Orange and gold swathed its slopes, the poplar and maples and hickories each adding its brilliant hues. October in all its mountain splendor, with a hint of frost in the air each night and a promise of more than frost before too long.

The horse pricked up his ears as she made him turn off the main wagon-road into a side trail that led upward toward the main lead of Wildcat. She noticed the change in the animal and figured it must be the right trail. The gelding stopped a hundred yards up the trail and stared intently up the mountain, its ears swiveling back and forth, then it continued. She knew then it had to be the right trail, the animal's behavior meant that another horse was somewhere up ahead.

They climbed to the top of the first finger-ridge, then upward toward the lead, the spine of Wildcat Mountain. Twice she heard an owl hoot, too loud and too early in the afternoon for a real owl.

"Whur ya' goin'?"

The mixed-blood Cherokee suddenly appeared in the trail, jumping out at her from behind a huge hemlock, grabbing her horse's bridle reins.

His voice was gutteral, almost a grunt, but his face showed no emotion at all, only deep black eyes staring into hers.

"Kirkwood," she squeaked out, startled by the Indian. "I'm looking for Tobe Kirkwood."

"Keep goin', top o' th' mountain."

She passed another guard, alerted by the Indian's owl-hooting, who stared at her and said nothing. The gelding picked his way among some large boulders as the trail wound higher. Finally they arrived on a flat, wooded, but fairly level place atop the ridge.

Through the trees she could see horses picketed and her own mount whinnied at them. She smelled woodsmoke and saw men seated on rocks around a small fire. They looked in her direction, but showed no signs of alarm. She rode up to the fire and looked them over, ragged rough men who stayed in the woods away from the war's uniforms and battlefields and fought in their own fashion, sometimes for a cause, sometimes just for themselves.

She recognized Big Tobe Kirkwood immediately, his red hair and beard were prominent, his manner was even more so. From the way he got up and walked over to hold her horse's bridle, he was obviously in command of this outfit and it showed.

"Who are ya', little girl?" he said confidently. "What do ya' want, what are ya' doin' here?"

"I saw you in town," she started, then suddenly became nervous and found herself grasping for words. "I-I-I just want...I-I mean I wanted to see you an-an-an..."

"Tobe, y've skeered her to death," his men taunted. "Let her get down and have some coffee, maybe she'll get over it."

Smiling at her, she couldn't tell whether it was real or arrogance, he offered his hand and she climbed down from the gelding. One of the other bushwhackers tied her horse to a tree for her.

"Thanks," she managed, as they handed her a rusty cup of foul- smelling coffee. Real coffee was a thing of the past, this late in the War, so this version was apparently made from roasted oats and scorched acorns. It was bitter and strong.

"My, that's bad," she said. "Whenever this War gets over, I bet real coffee will sell good everywhere, I can't wait to taste real coffee again."

They all laughed and one of them patted her on the shoulder. She recognized two of the guerillas as youths she had gone to school with in the years before the War.

"Y'er Buck Rose's girl, ain't ya'?" one of them said now. "I mind goin' t' school with you. Hattie June Rose, ain't that y'er name?" She nodded and they spoke of her father, several had known him.

"Well, Miss Hattie June Rose, y'aint told us whut y'er doin' out here," Kirkwood said, from his seat across the fire from her. They had rolled small boulders into a ring which surrounded the fire and Kirkwood presided from his rock-seat, which was at the base of a big oak. His eyes were intent on her now.

"My daddy got killed, got hanged by the Yankees," she said, looking into their faces. "They come from somewhere down on Shoal Creek. It burns me up that they done him like that and I want to kill 'em all, so I want to join up with y'all."

"Naw," Kirkwood spat, shaking his head immediately. "We don't need no girls, go on back home, get away from here."

"Aw, Tobe, let'er stay," one of her former schoolmates said. "Maybe she kin cook fer us, be better'n whut we cook. Let'er stay."

"No, she ain't stayin'. Go home, girl."

"Mister Kirkwood, I saw you ride through town and they told me you were shot to pieces by the Yanks and you still lived. They say you got spunk and you hate Yankees and that's enough for me," she pleaded earnestly now. "I beg you to let me stay. Like he says, I can cook and sew and keep the camp for you, but I can do lots more than that. I want to see all these Yankees dead, specially on Shoal Creek , the ones that hanged my Dad. I can go into these towns on Saturdays, when they all come to market, and talk to folks and spy for you. Find out who's helping the Yanks and tell y'all about it."

Kirkwood was wavering now and she could tell it, pressing her case.

"Who'd suspect a girl? I can talk to old women, who gossip and know everything. You can't, none of you can."

Kirkwood stroked his glossy red beard thoughtfully and rubbed his head, looking around into the faces of his men. Tired of poor cooking and anxious for a female voice once in a while, they missed the comforts of home and were, to a man, in favor of the girl.

"We'll let ya' stay fer a little while, I guess," Kirkwood said and the men whooped in joy, shaking Hattie June's hand with glee. "But if I don't like it, after a while y'll have to go back."

They unsaddled her horse for her and brought the saddle and bag of clothing and food to her.

"I'll fix supper," she announced. "I'll show you how handy I am."

With her old schoolmates helping her, Hattie June began to bustle around the fire and cook a meal for the dozen bushwhackers. Kirkwood grinned at the activity, but stood aside and watched.

"Get some wood," she ordered her helpers."Get the fire built up a little more. Bring water and some mud."

They never questioned, but jumped to do her bidding. She produced a number of fresh potatoes from her sack and put one of the youths to wrapping each one in a sticky coat of mud.

"Now put 'em in the coals and let 'em bake," she said. "Y'all got any meat?"

They had half a hog carcass hanging in a nearby tree and with her butcher-knife, she cut off several strips from one of the hams, then cut the strips into smaller pieces.

"This old fryin' pan's all we got, Hattie," one of the youths said then. "Kin ya' make do with it?"

She nodded and filled the pan with ham slices, putting it on the fire, too. Soon the smell of frying ham filled the camp, mixing with the aromatic woodsmoke. With the autumn leaves on the trees adding their soft colors, it was a peaceful scene, almost a picnic.

"We ain't got no plates, Hattie. Ever' man's got a knife and we just usually eat with 'er hands and 'er knife blades."

"Don't worry, I brought y'all something. Look here."

From her food sack, Hattie brought forth cornbread, fresh cornbread baked on the hearth that very day. Two big pones of it, flat and round and hefty as a chunk of wood.

Every man in camp, Kirkwood included, stared at the cornbread and thought of his own womenfolk at home, mothers or sweethearts or sisters and their mouths began to water. All eyes were on her and they listened to her orders without any doubt, her voice for the moment becoming the tongue of home-women they had obeyed in the past, the domestic authority of house and hearth.

"Put these pones on that rock there and one of you, the one with the cleanest knife, cut them into equal portions. Each man get one piece of cornbread, cut it open with your own knife and put a piece of ham from that pan in it. Each man also gets one potato, the mud will shell right off of it. Y'all can drink sp ring water or some more of that awful coffee."

After supper they thanked her for the meal and then sat around the fire and talked, spinning great stories for her benefit, to show their bravery and cunning. Kirkwood told his share, too, ending with the big fight on the Nottley.

"Boys, we took Athens like pickin' an apple, by God, took all th' hosses and mules, took stuff outta the stores. Thought we got away clean, but they hit us at dawn the next day, killed ever' man and 'bout killed me, too."

***

She rolled out her blanket on a spot not far from the fire and fell asleep to the sound of their talking. So far they had all treated her like a lady, she thought, but she slept with the butcher-knife under the blanket's edge and her daddy's pistol in the saddle bags, in easy reach.

She awoke in the wee hours of the morning, with the cool damp night air on her face. There was a movement beside her, something or somebody was lifting the blanket, letting in the cool air and trying to lie down beside her. She felt a rough hand grab her around the waist and then move upward to grasp her breast. She fought like a cat, twisting and turning, then grabbing under the corner of the blanket for the greasy butcher-knife, her old friend from home.

"Y'er sleepin' in my camp, woman, I want some pussy from you," Kirkwood grunted, trying to pin her down with his weight. "Hush now, y'll wake ever'body up."

Her hand found the knife now and she pressed the point upward into his belly. He felt the pressure and suddenly relaxed his grip on her, knowing a weapon was in play now.

"That's right, big boy, that's the knife that I cut up the meat with tonight. And, by God, I'll cut off yore meat with it, if you don' leave me alone. Get away."

"Y'er a feisty little thang, Hattie, but my time'll come with you."

"It might, and then again, it might not. Time'll tell. But don't ever come up on me in the dark again like that, mister. I don't like that, not one little bit."

He backed away from her and went back to his

side of the fire and she lay awake for a long time and thought about her choices. She could leave at daylight and be back home with Little Buck and Granny in a few hours, or she could stay with this band of desperate men, cooking for them and spying for them, and sooner or later she would be taken by one or more of them. She knew that, Granny had said it before she left. Now, Kirkwood had showed her, plain and simple, what lay ahead of her.

He was the leader. If she became his woman, at least she would have power over the others and would not have to submit to any of them. It would be his power, but she could command them and they would do her bidding. And most of all, dear Lord most of all, she wanted vengeance on the horrible Yankee people.

Nothing else mattered.

Other girls in school had spoken little of sex, Granny had told her little of it, but if other women could endure it then she could too. She vaguely hoped she did not get a child, but put that thought out of her mind.

To kill Yankees, to bring war on Shoal Creek, she would sleep with Kirkwood when the time came. Soon, if he desired it. And she would gain a certain power over him, would be able to bend him to her will, too.

***

"Fix us some breakfast, Hattie June, I'm a hungry man," he said next morning, grinning at her as if nothing had happened. "I could eat a horse."

"The captain's a-courtin' Hattie June," the men whispered to each other and laughed. He had no rank, but some of them referred to Kirkwood as their captain. "He'll get her, bye-an-bye."

They walked among the picketed horses and then

out to the top of the ridge, to get a little space between them and the camp.

"I want ya', girl, I can't have you buckin' me like ya' done last night and stayin', an' if y're gonna stay here, then I aim to have ya' tonight, fer sure."

She looked at him and blinked, thinking about the bargain, to stay would mean to submit.

"Ya' say ya' hate Yankees, Hattie June, I'll show ya' somethin'." He took off his shirt and stood bare-chested before her, letting her look fully at the pink scars still healing, scabs still on one wound.

"Lookit that, look at the side of my head, half m'ear's gone, fer God's sake. Look what they done to me. Ya' think I don't hate ever' damn one of 'em?"

He was shaking with rage now and emotion and her heart felt pity and sorrow for this red-headed boy-man, only a few years older than she was, his pale white skin outraged by Yankee lead, scars he would carry forever.

He reached out his arms and she went into his embrace. They hugged tight together and stood there for a long time.

"I want to be married before we do anything."

"Married?!?"

"Yes, married. You're not supposed to do things like that 'til you get married."

"Good God, woman, I don't need no wife."

"Well, then, you don't need me."

"Hell, we ain't got no preacher anyhow. I'm a guerilla, we're in a war, y'oughta know that…"

"We don't need a preacher. Just take me to a church and we'll stand there together and hold hands and say we're married. We'll marry ourselves."

He laughed like a wild man and then gave a rebel yell that shook the woods. "Ay God, boys, mount up," he yelled, putting his shirt back on hurriedly. "We gonna ride off and get married."

With whoops and shouts, they saddled their horses and Hattie's too and a few minutes later, all rode out of camp down the back side of the mountain, following the red-headed chief.

They rode hard for 20 minutes and came out in a clearing where a small unpainted church stood, surrounded by crude hand-hewn tombstones of a tiny cemetery. The front door was secured with a brass padlock.

"They ain't got no preacher on 'count o' th' War," Kirkwood said. "They don't use this place much no more. Shoot the lock off, boys." With several pistol shots, they ruined the padlock and it fell onto the front steps of the church, the door now riddled with bullet holes.

"Ready, Hattie?" Kirkwood asked, offering his hand to help her dismount. Hattie was having trouble holding her mount steady, the horse not accustomed to gunfire.

"I'm ready if you are, Tobe." It was the first time she'd spoke his name and they both got the message of acceptance it meant.

Hand-in-hand they entered the dusty little chapel and walked down the aisle to the altar.

His men stayed outside, still mounted on their horses.

"Well, Hattie, we're here. What do we say?"

"Let's just say we're married, man and wife from now on."

"All right, we're married then. Does it suit you?"

"Yes, we're married."

He turned and embraced her and kissed her clumsily and then, almost as an afterthought, patted her strongly on the rump.

"Wait right here," he said. "I'm gonna go get a blanket and have the honeymoon right here, right now."

"What?!"

"Yeah, right here, right now. Y'er m'wife now, ya' have to listen to what I say."

"Let's wait until tonight, when it gets dark."

"Naw, cain't wait. Stand right there."

He ran out the door, jerked the saddle off his horse and brought the saddle-blanket back with him, closing the door behind him.

"Now, Hattie June Rose, we'll really be man and wife."

He threw the blanket, still warm with animal heat and reeking of horse odor, on the floor and began to take off his clothing, grinning at her and glancing at the windows. His men were at each window, straining to see through the dusty glass panes.

Hattie smiled at him, so excited over having her. It was a strange feeling, to have this effect on a man, it made her feel strong. She unbuttoned her clothing and let it fall away, slowly peeling off each piece.

When she stood nude before him, Kirkwood attacked her, forcing her backward onto the smelly saddle-blanket on the floor.

"By God, he's topped'er now, look at that, boys."

They fought for viewing space at the windows, each pressing his face against the windows for a better look. Frantically they wiped at the dirty windows, but most of the dust was on the inside of the glass and their swiping with coat-sleeves and dirty handkerchiefs did not help at all.

It was not pleasant, Hattie thought, but it could be endured. Kirkwood grunted and plunged and poked inside her body and her mind was now simply elsewhere, wandering the fields of home with Little Buck or helping Granny do some chore.

She was in no danger, she knew that. She had something this man wanted and this gift could be used to her advantage, to give her power over him. In a minute or two it was over and he got up off her, looking strangely grateful.

***

Saturday morning dawned cool and rainy and she rode toward Murphy, accompanied by the two bushwhackers she had known as a child. Kirkwood gave her some money to buy food with and sent her to market, staying in camp.

"Gimme a big kiss 'fore ya' go," he ordered, kissing her full on the mouth to the cheers of the men. "Remember whose woman y'are," as he patted her publicly on the tail.

She smiled patiently at his crude display of affection and rode away with her escorts.

"F'ar that pistol just one time and we'll come a-runnin' if ya' need us," they said. They tied their horses in the woods near the river and let her proceed alone into the main street ,where the market activity took place in the open wagons and along the dirt street.

Hattie mixed freely with the people, as she had done all her life here. Many knew her and she knew them, none knew yet of her relationship with the dreaded Kirkwood Bushwhackers. She spoke with two of her cousins, then an old friend of Granny's, then several of the Home Guard who had known her father Buck. Constantly she eavesdropped on other conversations, picking up a bit here and a bit there.

She bought some corn meal, at a high price, and some apples. It all went into a sack, tied to her saddle-horn, and soon they were safely back at camp.

"What news? What did you find out?" Kirkwood asked.

"The war news is the same, no good, the South is still holding on, but we're pressed on every side."

"I know all that, how 'bout 'roun here?"

"I did hear one thing, about a man on Shoal Creek."

"Tell us, girl, tell us."

"There's a man on Shoal Creek who's got a boy in the Union army. They say he's bought a brand-new saddle from a peddler-man and got it hanging up on his front porch. Say's he's gonna send it to his boy. The man's name is Wilson and he's a blacksmith, well-known and easy to find. They told me directions to his place."

"Got a saddle hanging on his porch, does he? Sounds mighty bold fer a Yankee in these parts. Le's go visitin' down that way soon's this rain lets up."

"I didn't know whether you'd want to ride that far for a saddle or not."

"Sure, girl, sure. Besides, if he's a blacksmith we kin make 'im shoe my hoss and yours too, before we take the saddle. An' we kin take anything else he's got that we want."

"I want to see if he knows who hanged my Papa, too."

"These Indians'll make 'im talk. You'll know, if he knows anything ta tell."

They took eight men in all, the two Indians included, and rode into Shoal Creek early in the morning. James Wilson's house and shop were easy to find.

"I need my hoss shod," Kirkwood told him.

The man looked around at Hattie and the others, suspicious, but saying nothing. He heated the shoes in his fire, beat them with a hammer to fit the hooves and tacked them into place. Kirkwood's horse was soon shod, stamping its hooves impatiently.

"Now hers," Kirkwood grunted and the blacksmith began work on Hattie June's horse. The other bushwhackers remained seated on their mounts, watching the little drama unfolding.

Kirkwood and Hattie remained on the ground, walking around and looking over the shop and the house beside it. Wilson's wife was apparently inside cooking, they could smell the woodsmoke and sometimes hear the rattle of pots and pans. Two old hounds had barked at them as they rode up and then retreated under the house. It was quiet except for the melodic ringing of the hammer on the anvil, bending each shoe to fit the particular hoof it was going on.

"I'll have my pay now, for two horses," Wilson said when it was finished, handing Hattie the reins to her horse.

"We don't pay f'er work don' by Yankees," Kirkwood sneered, suddenly bringing a cocked revolver up from underneath his coat. "You mind y'er manners er some lead's gonna be yore pay."

Wilson stood his ground, eyeing the pistol in his face, and the mounted bushwhackers laughed in glee, kneeing their horses to move in closer on him until he was surrounded by howling guerillas looking down at him.

"Tie 'im up," Kirkwood ordered. "Tie 'im to that post there."

In a flash, Wilson was tied with some of his own rope and securely fastened to a post that held up the roof of the blacksmith shop. Kirkwood nodded to one of the Indians to come closer, so Wilson could not hear the orders.

"Hattie here wants to know if he was in the bunch that killed her pa, or if he knows anything about it. Use y'er knife, do whatever it takes."

The mixed-blood Cherokee walked over to the tied-up Wilson and with no emotion at all on his dark flat face drew a wicked-looking bowie from his belt sheath and brought the point up under the victim's chin. Feelings rising up inside her, Hattie ran to the helpless man and screamed with hate right in his face.

"You Shoal Creek murderers killed my daddy, Buck Rose. Were you there when they did it?"

Wilson's eyes rolled back and forth, from the Indian's face to the wild countenance of the girl. He shook his head, too frightened to speak.

"If you didn't do it, do you know who did?"

"No, no," he finally managed to speak. "I didn't have nothin' to do with it, not me."

"Then do you know who did?"

He hesitated to speak again and it was plain he knew something he had not told yet.

"He ain't tellin' it all," Kirkwood said, chuckling at the Indian. "Split his jaw for 'im, Greybeard, let 'im know we're serious." The knife moved upward from under the chin to press directly on the jawbone. The Indian made a quick move and the tip of the blade slashed down through the whiskers to the bone, leaving a bleeding incision of about two inches in length.

Wilson groaned at the sudden pain and felt his own warm blood coursing down the side of his throat into his shirt collar. Wild-eyed with fear, he began to babble.

"It was them Bradfords. They said they was the ones that done it. I never did it, never knew nothin' about it. The Bradfords brought a bunch o' corn back with 'em after they done it, said that old man wouldn't be a-needin' it. They live on the lower end o' th' creek, near the Tennessee line."

They untied him from the post then and let him stand there, blood still running down from his cheek wound.

"That's a right purty saddle on y'er porch there, we'll be takin' it now," Kirkwood said, sending one of the younger men to get it.

"Now, just a minute," Wilson said. The saddle intended for his son was his property and he got mad at the nerve of these bushwhackers taking it. So mad that he forgot his cut face and the words flowed.

"Y've got no right to take my saddle, I paid f'er it and it's mine. I wish some soldiers'd come by and settle things around here."

"What kind o' soldiers you favor, Confederate er Yankee?" Kirkwood taunted him.

"Don't matter," Wilson shot back. "Y'er stealing my stuff. That's against God's law, one o' th' Commandments. Rebel or Yankee, stealin' ain't right."

"I think we'll just take you and the saddle both," Kirkwood said. "Let ya' walk all the way back to town and tell the Home Guard y'er story. Usually I'd kill ya' myself, but they might like to hear you."

They tied him to a bushwhacker's saddle with a long length of rope and started back toward Murphy, Wilson walking as fast as he could to keep up. His wife, sensing what was happening, ran out crying as they left, but a pistol shot over her head sent her scampering back into the house.

"Let her cry," Hattie said, surprised at her own fierceness. "I cried when they killed my daddy. Let her cry."

"Y'er gettin' tough, girl," Kirkwood said. "Never thought my own wife would be so hard on folks." He was grinning now and she knew he was kidding her about the marriage. "Y'er a bushwhacker's woman now."

A mile from his house, Wilson jerked the rope loose from the guerilla's saddle and ran back down the trail. A hail of pistol bullet struck around him as he ran, two of them striking his body and knocking him to the ground. He scrambled up and ran into the thick laurel then, hidden from further gunfire.

"He's hit hard and he'll go for home," Kirkwood said. "Go git 'im quick, Greybeard, we'll wait."

The Cherokee nodded and dismounted. On moccasin-clad feet, he moved silently back down the trail and soon picked a spot where he knew the wounded man must cross. The rest of the bushwhacker gang rode off noisily and stopped to rest at a creek, where the horses could water.

Hearing them leave gave Wilson more confidence. He was hurt bad, but if he could just get back home, he might have a chance. His hands were still bound, but after several minutes of silence, he got to his feet and staggered through the woods.

He found the trail deserted and soon began to run forward in a jerky motion, moaning in pain and talking to his wife, hoping to reach home.

"Oh, Salina, darlin', help me! Help me!"

But the figure he saw in front of him as he rounded a sharp curve on the trail was not his beloved Salina. It was the Indian and he was holding that big knife again. Wilson shook his head to clear his vision. Was that really the Indian?

"No, no!" he roared at the vision in front of him.

Greybeard grabbed the wounded man by the throat with his left hand, and with his right, plunged the blade to the hilt into Wilson's heart.

Chapter Four

"You ought not to keep that saddle."
"Well, woman, I took it fair-an-square an' I like it."
"You should turn it in to the Home Guard or let the reg'lar Confederates have it when they pass through."
"Naw, I like it, think I'll keep it and ride on it. You kin hav' m'old saddle."
"I don't want it, Tobe, I want a lady's side-saddle rig someday."
"We'll get ya' one then, right away."
"You ought to give that Yankee saddle to the Home Guard."
"I ride f'er the South, too, woman, got just as much right to it as them."

She shook her head, disappointed that the trophy went not to the cause, but for Kirkwood to put on his own horse. Still, he had gotten out of Wilson some solid information for her on Buck's killers. He had confirmed that it was, indeed, the Bradfords from Shoal Creek. She'd find them, no matter how long it took.

They raided several times more, to liberate a repeating rifle from a Union man, or to take a crib full of corn from a Yankee soldier's family farm. They killed in almost every incident, Kirkwood executing people with a single pistol-shot to the face.

The drifters and the lay-outs who stayed in the woods to flee Confederate conscription officers joined them, plus deserters from both sides. The Kirkwood Bushwhackers soon numbered nearly thirty men.

***

Word spread of Hattie Rose and her bushwhacker lover. The Unions trembled when they saw her in Murphy, but the Rebs rejoiced in the victories of Buck Rose's daughter and told her everything, even riding out to the camp to sometimes talk with the dark-haired girl and tell her of Union treachery nearby.

"You don't talk a lot about yourself," she asked him on one warm November day in camp. "Pour me another cup of that awful coffee and tell me things. For example, I know you're not from around here."

They sat on two rocks near a low fire and sipped coffee, the mountain girl and the red-headed butcher, and talked to each other.

"I'm from up in East Tennessee, whur it's really rough. It really ain't too bad aroun' here, and it's real purty down here, I like it. I don't hav' to be from here, I kin always get somebody like you'ns to guide me or tell me how to get around."

"Were you in the army?"

"Hell, woman, I'uz in both of 'em," he laughed. "The Rebel army and the Yankee army. Jined the Rebs first and wore a reg'lar uniform and fit all over Virginny. Seen a lot o' men die, got disgusted and come home."

"You deserted from the Confederate Army?"

"Ya might say it that way. Deserted from the Unions, too. Joined th'r army last year up above Knoxville f'er the bonus pay they giv' ya' f'er signin' up. Lots done it. Left in about three days, but kept th'r money."

"Started bushwhackin' then?"

"Yeah, rode with a wild feller name of Champ Ferguson. Burnt a lot o' Union houses and killed a lot of 'em. Champ Ferguson learnt me a lot."

Opening up now, he began to talk more than usual, flattered by his pretty listener. He told her war stories of riding with the legendary Ferguson, of whom she had never even heard, of burning homes, and about women and children turned out into the night, their men shot down in front of them. She listened, fascinated, and realized that this strange, violent man she held captive between her legs in the darkness was not like other men at all. He was unpredictable, given to random acts of sheer terror, and human life – anyone's life – meant absolutely nothing to him.

Her power over him, however limited, was interesting to her. She pondered over what she could make him do, and what he would not do for her.

He could be kind, sometimes. He would bring her food or coffee, or find another blanket for her on the colder nights, but she could not make him give up the saddle or the fine rifles that he stole; they did not really go to help the South.

It was true what people said about him, he was a bushwhacker and a thief. True, he hated Yankees and did horrible things to them, but he sometimes robbed Southern sympathizers, too, even Rebel soldiers home on furlough, if they had something he wanted.

"I got one set o' kin-people not too fur from here," he volunteered. "My uncle and his wife live on a farm down toward Cleveland. We might jus' ride down and see 'em."

"Aren't you afraid of the Yankee soldiers?"

"Naw, they'll never catch us."

"But there's a bunch o' Yankees stationed now in Cleveland."

"We aint' gonna go all the way to Cleveland, Tennesssee, girl. We'll take a few men with us and slip in and out 'fore they know we're there."

"That red har of yours makes you easy to spot," she said. "And it scares people, too. We ought to take advantage of that, get a big red horse for you to ride, maybe even some red dogs. That way when we rode into a town, it would really get people's attention.

"Yeah, we need some dogs around this camp. Maybe if you'd had some dogs that time on the Nottley, the Yanks might not have slipped up on you so easy."

He had to agree. Woman or not, she was right. The bushwhackers had proved to be too careless about guards at night. Kirkwood had tried to instill some discipline in them, but they were too independent and he had given up, stoical about his fate if the enemy came at night again.

"Bulldogs," he grunted. "That's the ticket, bulldogs. By God, I want somethin' that'll bite hell out o' people."

"Don't matter what kind, just so they bark when they hear somebody coming," Hattie said.

"Red bulldogs," he repeated. "With spike collars on 'em. I seen some like that at a rich man's house we hit up in East Tennessee last year. Them spike collars protect their throats from another dog and make 'em look mean. 'At's what I want, two like that."

"And I want a sidesaddle to ride on, like a real lady."

"We'll get 'em, Hattie. I'll get me a red hoss and you kin comb out my hair long and purty. I won't wear no hat when we ride into a town so people can see m'hair real good. It'll skeer hell out of 'em when they see all that red."

***

Twenty-five miles to the northwest, just across the line in Coker Creek, Tennessee, a man named Coleman Bryson put on his brand-new Union Army shirt and looked at himself in the mirror.
"Well, what do you think?"
"I think y're gonna get y'erself killed," his wife said drily. "The Rebs 'roun here don't think much o' Yankee blue."
"Well, I know better than t'wear it out in the open, but at least I'm a captain now in the Union Army. Gonna have my own company."
"If ya' live long enough."
"I'll live, you kin bet on that."
"Where's this company o' your'n comin' from, wh'r they gonna go?"
"Gettin' some from 'roun here, but most of 'em from over in N'th Ca'lina. Them boys over there are hot f'er the Union."
"The Home Guard at Murphy, I hear, is hot f'er the South. An'how, 'bout that Rebel bushwhacker Kirkwood? He's a mean one, they call 'im the red-headed butcher. Killed a lot o' Union people in East Tennessee and now he's holed up at Murphy."
"I ain't skeered of a damn bushwhacker," he said, admiring the captain's bars on his blue shoulders. *The gold trim on the shirt looks good,* he thought. *Wished they'd give me the rest of the uniform, but this will be enough to impress these country people.*

The Union officers at Knoxville had explained the process to him and gave him some papers and the shirt. He was to raise a company of men from his supporters and bring them to Knoxville, where they would be issued arms and uniforms and mustered into the regular Union Army. They would be then sent back to their home area to fight against the local Home Guards and bushwhackers. And he, Coleman Bryson, would be their commander.

Just across the state line into the mountains of neighboring North Carolina, he had found ready recruits. These sturdy mountain men had no use for the Confederacy or its goals, they owned no slaves and they loved the Union.

Always on the lookout for money, they had heard of the bonus pay given Union recruits and were ready to join. Some were mere boys, others older men and a surprising number were of military age, but had simply, like him, dodged the war so far.

"Coleman, we're f'er ye," they had told him in secret meetings at Beaverdam and Shoal Creek. "Bring us the Union papers and we'll j'ine and go with ye t' Knoxville."

Heartened by the enthusiasm of these fierce Carolina mountaineers, Coleman Bryson bragged about their military operations.

"When I get this bunch armed and ready, boys, we'll bring down Hell on th'r punkin-heads," he promised. "We'll raid, by God, that damn commissary they got at the Murphy jail-house. An' if that rebel bushwhacker Kirkwood kin be found, we'll scalp that red head o' his'n."

They cheered and stomped and Bryson felt a glow of pride in his leadership of these rough men. They patted him on the back and shook his hand and all were proud of their company's plans.

"I'll be back in a week or two, with the papers to sign you'uns up," he promised. "I'll send word over here what day and wh'ur to meet me. Hooray f'er the Union!"

"Hooray," they cheered and stomped some more and crowed for the victory they would surely win. "The Home Guard and Kirkwood better look out f'er us!"

***

It all started when a new preacher came to town, a good fire-breathing Baptist with a wife who wanted to change the world. Folks were not accustomed to regular worship during the war years, so they flocked to his services in Murphy.

And his wife began a sort of school, the first thing resembling a public school the mountain country had seen since the regular school closed early in the War.

"I'm not a real school teacher and this won't be a real school," she told the women, "but all the country people come to town on Saturdays. So we'll have school at the church on Saturdays, all day. Bring me the young ones and I'll try to teach them."

It was a loose arrangement, but it worked for a time. The wagons that came to town on Saturday mornings for trading and selling goods now brought children in numbers, for the school. The children went to school while the adults went about their usual activities.

"Granny, I don't wanna go back to school."

"Little Buck Rose, y'r gonna grow up ignorant, plumb stupid, if ya' don't go back. Here's yore old book, I saved it f'er you'ns."

This conflict was settled in a number of homes as

youngsters used to freedom from school were forced back into the classroom. The pastor' wife worked with all ages and soon had a routine for them on Saturdays, beginning with the youngest ones first.

"You little ones work on your spelling now," she would say and begin calling out the words to them. The older ones would watch and listen, until their lesson time came later in the morning.

They would also visit and talk with each other.

In this manner, Little Buck Rose met the Gardiner boy again. They had been schoolmates three years earlier, but had seen little of each other during the War. The Gardiner boy was two years older than Little Buck and, at fourteen, was almost a man.

"Yore sister still live with Tobe Kirkwood?"

"Yeah," Little Buck flushed with shame at the question, yet saw no way to dodge it. His sister's public role in the War embarrassed him, living with a bushwhacker. "She comes to see us sometimes, not much. She's still in the woods, I guess, out there with the bushwhackers."

"Ol' Kirkwood is a mean hoss, they say he'd kill ya' f'er y'r boots."

"Don't know. Never seen him but once. He rode by our house wher she wuz comin' to see us, but then he rode off, never said much, just 'how do you do' to me and Granny."

"Are they married t'each other?"

"They say they are, but I don't know how."

The Gardiner boy was polite, he did not use the term 'camp whore' which Little Buck had heard hissed in the streets more than once on market day, said loudly enough on purpose for him to hear. Granny had heard it a time or two and had laid a good cussing on a Union woman once, which had stopped it.

"They say the war is 'bout over," the Gardiner boy said one Saturday afternoon to Little Buck. School out, they were walking along the river in Murphy, tossing rocks in the water. "They say the South is whupped f'er sure, that Lincoln has won it, all done."

"I wish it wuz over," Little Buck said glumly. "My daddy got killed, my sister is gone with the bushwhackers, everything is all messed up."

"My mama says it's all been fought on account o' niggers."

"We ain't got none," Little Buck volunteered. "We never had no money to buy none."

"Us neither, never had one, never wanted one. Big farmers like th' Harshaws have got 'em. I see a few in town sometimes."

Little Buck nodded. The big Harshaw farm upriver from Murphy had the best bottom land around and several black families worked the crops, some of the women used for house servants. He had seen black men driving Harshaw wagons sometimes in town, but not often.

"My mama says it's a rich man's fight and the poor men are doin' all the dyin'," the Gardiner boy said. "They're makin' men fight that don't want to, don't want to fight at all. It ain't right."

Little Buck nodded in agreement with the older boy, who seemed very confident. Little Buck missed his own mother, but believed she would probably say the same things, if she were alive.

Granny was not sympathetic when he told her of the talk that night, recounting what the Gardiner boy had said.

"The War ain't over yet, boy," she said, fiery with Southern pride. "We ain't whupped yet. Yore daddy died a fighter f'er the South and y'ought t'be proud o' that.

"An' besides, ya' better be careful talkin' to that Gardiner boy. He's got some cousins on his mama's side o' the family that I know are sidin' with the North. I heered ol' Molly just today at market a-talkin on some of 'em."

Little Buck went to bed with his mind in a frazzle, it was hard to keep everybody satisfied, sometimes it was just so hard. He liked the Gardiner boy and he wished that he could somehow escape from this war.

***

"This here's my wife Hattie," Kirkwood said.

"Pleased to meet you, girl," the aunt and uncle said, smiling and shaking her hand. "Glad y'all came, come in an' eat with us."

The uncle, a country doctor, was alarmed to hear about Kirkwood's close call in the Nottley River battle and soon had him disrobing, to better check his wounds. The scars showed plainly, some of the pink scar-tissue still sensitive to touch. The uncle clucked and shook his head.

"Y'r lucky to be alive, that's all I got to say. Pure lucky."

They spent a full day at the big house near the Ocoee River.

"Aren't y'all afraid of the Feds in Cleveland, they got a bunch of soldiers stationed there now. Must be several hundred and they could ride up to Murphy and get rough on you."

"Naw," Kirkwood said, laughing at the notion. "They got guerilla and Home Guards and even reg'lar

Confeds to worry about in all directions. They ain't gonna get serious with us, might send a patrol up our way now and then, but probably nuthin' mor'n that."

The aunt took Hattie out to their big barn before they left and gave her a proper side-saddle.

"If y're to ride with our nephew, honey, you might as well do it right. I'm getting too old to ride, haven't used this thing in years." With Kirkwood helping her, Hattie got the girth adjusted and the rig securely fastened to her horse. Now she could sit like a true lady, one leg hooked over the funny horn, her plain skirt modestly arrayed over the side of the horse.

"Get a better skirt, honey, and a nice hat and you'll look fine.'

"Thank you, ma'am, it's been real nice visiting with y'all."

***

From the uncle's house, they rode into the very outskirts of Cleveland and from there north for 20 miles, raiding and stealing and taking. Two of Kirkwood's men had relatives in the area and from them they received intelligence on Union families and likely targets.

Victims pleaded with the Union garrison at Cleveland for assistance, but by the time a small patrol was sent out, seeking Kirkwood with great reluctance, the bushwhackers had ridden safely back into their mountain stronghold.

Hattie June got a black velvet skirt, taken from a prosperous home north of Cleveland and a hat with a big feather in it. They had located two red bulldogs, at her urging, and forced a blacksmith to make matching spike collars for the dogs, using harness strap from his own shop.

The wealthy farm they had raided, and killed the owner, had also provided Kirkwood with the red horse Hattie wanted for him. A big gelding, it was a light red in color which truly matched the red beard and hair of the bushwhacker chief.

Dressed out in their new finery, they made a grand entrance back into Murphy. Some of the men rode in first, then came Kirkwood and Hattie June and the red bulldogs.

She had combed out his fine red hair and made him take his hat off. He rode the red horse arrogantly and she rode a step or two behind, in her new black riding skirt and hat with the plume.

"The red-headed beast and the queen o' the bushwhackers," snarled a Union man on the sidewalk to his mousy wife. "Trash if I ever seen it. By God, I hope Bryson gets both of 'em."

But he was shaking inside as he said it, watching the sleek red bulldogs and the dark-haired girl on the sidesaddle rig. Their theatrical entrance would be repeated time and time again until it became a part of mountain lore and legend, striking terror into the townspeople who witnessed it.

Big Tobe Kirkwood and Hattie June Rose, an unholy pair escorted by thirty armed riders, totally committed in the no-quarter guerilla war that raged through the Southern Appalachians.

Old Molly, Granny's gossipy friend, stopped them before they got to the jail and motioned for Hattie to get down. Two of the riders were ordered to stand guard with her while she spoke to the informant, while Kirkwood and the rest continued on to the jail.

"Hattie, it's Coleman Bryson," she said breathlessly. "He's off Six-Mile, over on Coker Creek, and he's a bad Union and he's a-gatherin' a full company o' men. Says he's gonna come to Murphy an' whup the Home Guard an' hang Tobe Kirkwood."

***

The Home Guard heard of Bryson's bragging, too, and put their spies to work. Along with Old Molly's pipeline, which worked through two cousins and a friend, the information soon flowed toward Murphy. It came in pulses, a message every few days or so.

Hattie rode to town daily now, escorted by several Kirkwood men. She called on Old Molly each time, then went to the jail to confer with the Home Guard. She was recognized as Kirkwood's lieutenant and respected as such.

"We got the word today," the Home Guard captain told her. "Reckon you'ns heard, too, from Old Molly." She nodded.

"We'll give you'uns extry powder and lead, such as we've got, but we're gonna let Kirkwood do the fightin' this time. We're too few and too old, we better stay in town. He's mad too, ain't he?"

"Yeah, Tobe's mad, madder'n a wet hornet. That Coleman Bryson's been strutting and bragging that he's strong enough to take Murphy and hang Tobe. We'll fix him, you just wait and see."

With a sack full of lead balls and a small wooden keg of powder given them by the Guard, Hattie and her escort rode back to the woods.

"It's all set for next Thursday, right in the middle of the week," she told Kirkwood. "Saturday is mostly the day people travel an' trade, so they're planning it this way on purpose, so nobody will know. Most folks will be at home, not on the roads, nobody will see what's going on 'til it's all over and done."

"Where at?"

"Evans Mill, down on Beaverdam Creek. They gonna gather there real early in the morning. Bryson's gonna come over from Tennessee with a couple of reg'lar Yankee officers and swear in the whole bunch. Then they're going to Knoxville, to be trained for a few days and given guns. They plan to come back then and rule the country around here."

Kirkwood grinned at the thoughts in his head; this information collected for him by this pretty girl was like gold. He could use it to destroy this budding rebellion. Plotting a good ambush was like a game to him and he had learned from cruel experience through the War.

"Who knows about the mill? About the country down there?"

"The Foster boys, those two I went to school with that have been with you so long, you know?"

"Bring 'em here, I want to know about the mill."

The Foster brothers, who had known Hattie since childhood and now rode with her in common cause, were eager to tell what they knew.

The mill, they said, was shut down because of the War. It was a two-story log structure beside Beaverdam Creek, they said, with a small pond behind it. The wheel did not run and it was now merely a convenient landmark, a small settlement of houses around it, maybe five houses in all.

"It's way out in the mountains from here," one of the Fosters said. "People 'roun' there took th'r corn and wheat there to be ground f'er meal an' flour before the War. Purty good road to it, not far from Tennessee."

***

That night in their blankets, he was rough with her. She submitted to his pawing and strong lunges and was glad when it was over. She could tell his mind was on the coming fight.
"Tobe, do you reckon any of the Bradfords that killed my Papa will be there?"
"I wondered when ya'd get aroun' t'askin' that," he said. "May be. If they do show up, we'll let ya' hav' em. I got a plan, tell you'uns about it in the mornin'."

***

Coleman Bryson was wearing his blue Union captain's shirt, with the gold braid showing plainly in the sunlight. He was striding up and down in front of the crowd, waving his arms and shouting about something. Kirkwood watched through a stolen spyglass from the woods a quarter-mile away and grinned.
"He's a-preachin' now, boys, lettin' em know how he's gonna rule the roost. Time f'er th' party to start."

***

The two bored Union officers stood off to one side, disgusted at Bryson's speech-making and boasting. They had his muster-list and were ready to administer the oath to these recruits, who stood spellbound at Bryson's crude oratory.
A total of two dozen men had showed up and they could be a formidable force under Bryson, especially if well-mounted and well-armed, which they were not.

Some had horses, but most of them had walked to the rendezvous. Most had rifles, but the officers noted that several of the pieces were antique flintlocks, unreliable and no match for the cap-and-ball rifles both North and South were using in the War. Two men had no weapons at all and there were only three pistols in the whole crowd.

Nor were there any pistols among Kirkwood's men hidden in the loft of the mill above them. The red-headed leader had distributed guns himself before they left their final camp and they were going entirely by his plan.

"We may be outnumbered, we may not, but we kin surprise th'r asses and kill hell out of 'em a'fore they know what's up," he told them. 'Listen and, by God, listen good t'me."

With fresh powder and caps supplied by the Home Guard, they had loaded all their rifles and the six men who sneaked into the loft well before daylight had carried three rifles apiece into their sniper nest.

"When the shootin' starts, have them guns wh'r ya' kin f'ar one and snatch up another'un," he said. "Ye'll be shootin' down on 'em and them runnin', some may get off a little distance.

"I'll bring about half with me and the Foster boys'll lead the other half. Ev'r'bdy on hosses have two pistols loaded and ready, two more loaded and ready in the saddle bags, if we kin find that many pistols among us. Them on hosses will be shootin' close, ride 'em down and shoot hell out of 'em. It'll be over in a minute, I g'arantee."

***

The diabolical ambush, Bryson would observe, worked to perfection. Horrible realization crept closer and unfolded on itself before his eyes. He was still speaking, telling his new troops what they would all do to Murphy when he first noticed the sound of horses approaching. Gladdened by the thought of more recruits, his jaw dropped as the horsemen suddenly spurred into a gallop. Then he heard more horses from the opposite direction, also coming hard.

Bryson's head jerked from side to side as he looked, he could not resist looking at the two squads of horsemen bearing down on them. Each reaction took a few seconds and the speed of the horses brought them that much closer. Some of Bryson's recruits started to run and then a strange sound, a scuffling and knocking noise from above, startled them all and they all paused for a second or two to look up.

The shuttered windows of the mill loft were being kicked open from inside, a noisy dusty racket that ended before their eyes with a gang of bearded bushwhackers appearing on the window-sills above with their rifles.

"It's Kirkwood," yelled one, the recruit recognizing the red hair and beard of the lead rider. "Run, boys!"

The rifles in the loft above began firing immediately, their first two targets the blue-uniformed Yankee officers, now running for their own horses. The first lead slug took flesh and the Union officer screamed and fell in the dirt road grasping frantically at his lower back. Shot through the bowels, he writhed in agony and yelled in pain with ferocious volume for several seconds.

The second Union actually got into the saddle. He had been hidden behind his horse for a moment in mounting and the sniper in the loft merely waited until his target swung up on the animal's back and then neatly shot the officer through both lungs, toppling him off on the road.

"Hey, hey, y'all don't leave," Kirkwood was laughing, taunting his victims. He rode among the fleeing men, the bridle in his teeth and a smoking pistol in each hand, firing point-blank into the bodies of the terrified recruits.

Two of the recruits stopped at the edge of the woods and turned to face the mill with their old guns. They fired, both missed, dropped their guns and ran like the rest. Bryson took a pistol ball through the shoulder and fled into the woods, his path noted by the bushwhackers. They rode into the woods, too, getting ahead of the fleeing recruits and cutting them off. They soon had them rounded up, at least most of them. Bryson escaped, temporarily.

"Count 'em up, what we got?" Kirkwood said.

They were doing the tally when Hattie rode up and looked over the carnage. She had seen one or two dead men in some of their homestead raiding, but she had never seen so many bodies and she had *never* actually witnessed a killing. That would change soon.

"We ain't lost a man, n'er even had one wounded, Tobe. Looks like seven o' th'rs dead in the road here, includin' th' two Unions. Bryson got away, but it looks like he's hit good. An' we captured twelve men."

Hattie's horse picked its way carefully through the dead bodies in the road and she looked over the prisoners, who glared at her. Most knew the stories of Kirkwood's woman.

"Tobe, don't shoot any more right now. I want to talk to some o these prisoners."

"Hattie's gonna get rough, I bet," he smirked. He knew what she wanted. "Boys, le's move this bunch into the woods a ways. I don't lik bein' out here in the open too long."

They hazed the sullen prisoners into the mountains, making them walk for a mile or more up the road toward Tennessee, then breaking off the road and going into virgin timber for another half-mile. Well off the road, they stopped in a hollow and Hattie picked out the two youngest prisoners for questioning. Both were little more than boys. *Barely sixteen-years-old,* she thought, *and plainly scared.* She thought of her father hanging in Old Man Tysinger's barn and felt herself stiffen.

The first youth was not much help. He said his name was Jones and he was crying so hard it was difficult to understand him. Hattie asked him if he knew any Bradfords from Shoal Creek and he looked at the other boy and then shook his head. One of the men slapped him hard then and he cried some more and said the other youth, who was being held out of earshot, he thought was a Bradford, but he wasn't sure. The recruits had been contacted individually by Bryson and mostly were not acquainted with each other.

"Bring th'other. This un's no good," Kirkwood growled.

The second boy was plainly nervous, twitching his legs and rubbing his eyes. Kirkwood was growing disgusted with the questioning, he wanted it over with so they could take up the trail of the wounded Bryson. Three of his mixed-blood Cherokees, led by Greybeard, were trailing Bryson now and Kirkwood wanted to rejoin them as soon as possible.

"Boy, ya' know who I am?" he asked, cocking a pistol and pushing the muzzle roughly into the youth's eye-socket. "Ya' b'leeve I'll kill ya' right here?"

The youth wet his pants and began to cry, sobbing loudly. He managed to speak finally.

"Yessir, Mister Kirkwood, I know."

Hattie felt no compassion for him at all, she looked at him as she would a bug. Kirkwood withdrew the pistol and the boy began to blubber through his tears.

He was kin to the Bradfords, through his mother's side, but he had not been present at the hanging of Buck Rose and Old Man Tysinger. He knew who did it, four men, and he named three Bradfords and a Davenport.

Did he know where they were now? He paused for a moment and then begged for his life and one of the guerillas hit him on the head with a flint rock. He cried some more and finally told them that, as far as he knew, the Davenport had fled to Tennessee to join the Union and one of the guilty Bradfords had been among those shot down in front of the mill. Two others were among the prisoners now held by Kirkwood.

"Point'em out."

He indicated two young men, in their 20's, on the end of the line of prisoners. Kirkwood muttered an order and they were brought forward and tied to two trees.

"You the Bradfords that hanged two Home Guards a few months back?" he asked them curtly. They looked at Kirkwood and then at each other. Finally one spoke.

"Yeah we are and I'd say y'r gonna hang us now, ain't that right?"

Kirkwood did not answer them, turning instead to Hattie. "There they are, girl, what's left o' the four men who killed y'r pa. Do whatever you want with 'em."

Hattie approached the two, looking into their faces. They were young, only a few years older than she was, their dirty faces covered with scraggly beards.

"Who're you?" one asked.

"I know who ya' are," the other said quickly, the first time he had spoken. "Y're Hattie June Rose, Kirkwood's woman, and one of th' Home Guards we killed wuz y'r pa."

She felt no compulsion, no obligation to answer their comments or even to talk to them. Her mind was rushing, swirling with all sorts of thoughts. The sight of her father's body in the wooden coffin, an image of the two bodies hanging in the old barn, the tearful face of her brother Little Buck when he was told of his father's murder.

She was holding her father's pistol in her hand, the .36-caliber cap-and-ball that he had left at home the morning of his death, and now she leveled it at the two captives.

"Hurry up and get it over with," Kirkwood ordered her. "We need to get on Bryson's trail."

She stepped close now, so close she could see the hate in their young eyes and they could see it in hers, an animal sort of feeling, pure anger.

"You bitch from hell, I hope to God the devil gets you tonight," one said, cursing Hattie and straining at his ropes.

She thumbed the hammer back and pointed the gun at him, so close the muzzle almost touched his chest. She pulled the trigger, the gun bucked, spitting flame and smoke. His eyes bulged in pain and terror and she shot him again through the chest. His legs collapsed and the body fell against the sagging ropes.

She turned to the second, who stared and said nothing. She cocked the pistol again and deliberately placed the muzzle against his heart and fired. Their gaze locked, his eyes on hers and he stared until death glazed his eyes and he slid slowly down the tree, as far as the ropes would let him.

Trembling now with rage and emotion, Hattie turned to Kirkwood and sat down on a log before she spoke.

"Thanks, Tobe, for bringing me to 'em and letting me kill them."

"Ya' done good, girl," he grinned. "Blood f'er blood, that's the way, don't never forgit it."

***

Coleman Bryson ran as best he could, with the panic-stricken Ledford beside him and they thrashed through the laurel and around the side of the mountain like two frightened deer, going helter-skelter over logs and boulders in their flight.

Greybeard and the other two trackers winked at each other and smiled with glee. These two Union men were leaving a plain trail, one a child could follow with ease.

The broken limbs and turned-up leaves on the forest floor were easy to follow and the Indians soon sent one of their number back to the main road to bring the horses and follow the chase. When Kirkwood and Hattie and the rest came up the main road toward Tennessee, they soon found the Indian with the horses and joined the pursuit there.

It was plain that Bryson and Ledford were heading for Bryson's home on Coker Creek, just over the line into Tennessee. Kirkwood and his bushwhackers stayed on horseback on the main road, knowing that Greybeard and the other tracker were hot on their prey.

Bryson was almost fainting from loss of blood and fatigue, but he ran on. There was a list of all his supporters, people he counted on, in his coat at the cabin, these wolves must not get it. If only he could reach it and destroy it before they found it.

Ledford, who was not wounded, ran with him and sometimes helped him over the bad places, letting the crippled Union leader lean on him.

It was in a stance like this, working their way over some rocks very near Bryson's home that they first saw the two mixed-blood Cherokees close behind them.

The trackers saw immediately that their quarry was not armed and began to taunt them, giving Indian war-whoops and drawing their knives, waving them in the morning sunlight.

"Run," Ledford shouted. "I'll hold 'em off."

Bryson stumbled on and Ledford turned to face their pursuers. Kirkwood and company, hearing the Indian war-whoops, were dismounting and joining the chase now on foot.

The two Indians man-handled Ledford, knocking him to the ground and then tying him quickly to a tree. Then they sprinted to the fleeing Bryson, who had now reached the very yard of his cabin. One caught him from behind and, laughing with glee, reached around with his knife to Bryson's abdomen and slashed it open.

Still holding his wounded shoulder with his good arm, Bryson looked down in horror at his own pink entrails falling out of the bloody gash to the ground.

He went to his knees and on all fours, began to crawl into the cabin. Laughing maniacally now, the two Indians stood over him and one put the point of his knife into Bryson's shoulder and cut his back diagonally from shoulder to buttocks. Blood spurted onto the Union blue shirt and Bryson screamed in agony. The Indians howled and one kicked Bryson over onto his back.

He was reaching for a coat hanging on a peg on the wall with his good arm when they drove a bowie deep into his heart and more blood stained the shirt.

Moments later, Hattie and Kirkwood entered the cabin. The Indians were stripping the bloody shirt off Bryson and they pointed at the coat on the wall. Kirkwood went through the pockets quickly and found a sheet of paper with writing on it.

"Here, what's this?" he said, handing it to Hattie. She could read better than any of the bushwhackers.

"Looks like a list of his men."

"Well, we shore don't need that. Hell, we've already killed him and all his men. L'es go to Murphy, bring that man and we'll hang him on the Square in the middle o' town, let 'em know how we deal with th' Unions."

They had left the dead in the dust in front of Evans Mill, to be buried by citizens, some of whom had witnessed part of the massacre and would add to the legend of Kirkwood and his bushwhackers. There were another dozen men dead, executed in the woods, whose bodies strangely would never be found. Bryson's wife, who was away from the cabin, would return later that day to find her husband's body minus the shirt.

***

The Indians whooped and howled and rode up and down the streets of Murphy waving their trophy, Bryson's bloody captain's shirt. Ledford was hanged from a tree near the Square and Hattie rode to camp with Bryson's secret list of supporters in her saddle bags, to be looked at later.

Chapter Five

Little Buck Rose and the Gardiner boy were checking their rabbit traps, walking through the canebrakes along the Hiawassee River not far from the Rose home.

"Ain't many rabbits this year."

"Maybe we'll ketch more after Christmas, when it gits colder."

"Won't be much of a Christmas this year, will it?"

"Naw, Granny ain't got no money. Don't reckon I'll get much, maybe an apple."

"Me neither," the Gardiner boy said. "Times are shore hard."

They trudged on, Little Buck and his taller companion. They talked of school and the books they detested and the War.

"One o' my uncles is in the Army out West, fightin' Indians. Boy that'd be fun."

"Might be fun," Little Buck said. "But you ain't old enough to be in the Army."

"He's in the reg'lar American army, the Union Army," the Gardiner boy said. "An' I could be in the Army, too, as a drummer boy. You could too, they have real young boys for drummers."

"That would be fun," Little Buck blurted out, ashamed to be speaking of the Union Army, but suddenly overjoyed with the very thought of being somewhere else, away from this war in the South. "I bet they have purty uniforms and lots of good food to eat and nobody to fight 'cept ol' Indians."

***

The Yankee lieutenant looked idly at the country they were passing through, a rough rocky gorge with steep bluffs rising into the cold December air. The horses' breath made steam, an individual cloud of it swirling around each animal's head. They were good Union cavalry horses and well-shod, their steel shoes making the stones in the road ring with their passing.

He had fifteen men in the patrol, good sturdy troopers, each armed with the new Spencer repeater. They had received some training with the funny-looking rifles back in camp at Cleveland, consisting mainly of letting the men learn from each other how to best load and fire the lever-action weapons.

Now they loved the new gun, would not go back to their old slow single-shot muzzleloaders for anything. And anyone could see that a small group of men armed with Spencers would be equal to a much large body of troops armed only with muzzle-loaders.

"This looks like Colorado. I was stationed in the West and it reminds me of the country there," he said to the civilian guide.

"Don't know, never been West," the man said.

"Why is there such a good road out here in this gorge?"

"They dig copper ore up the road from here, bring it out in wagons down this road," the guide said. "'Er.. at least they did before the War. It's all stopped now."

They forded a small stream, coming down from a

hollow on the side of the gorge into the main river, and paused to water their horses. "What's the name of this place, this river here?"

"They call it the Ocoee. Indian name I guess."

The guide was nervous, he could see that, but the lieutenant was not. With fifteen good men behind him, well-mounted and well-armed, he feared nothing in the mountain country ahead of them.

There was supposedly a bushwhacker of some local note ahead of them, a red-haired guerilla who needed to be hunted down and killed, if possible. The guide was scared of this man and the guerilla had at least some small regional following.

"He's a desperado of the darkest dye," the old colonel had told him a few days back. "Lieutenant, I want you to take two squads and ride up there to Murphy and get him if you can. If you can't find him, report back to me as soon as possible and we may take even stronger actions."

The colonel said small reports of outrages against Union families had trickled in for several months, but it was getting worse. Now in the past weeks, this man Kirkwood had apparently ambushed a recruiting effort involving regular officers from Knoxville and a local Union leader named Bryson.

"The reports say he killed two enrollment officers and Captain Bryson and all his recruits," the colonel said. "A brazen and dastardly act, done in broad daylight. The man must be stopped. With the Spencers, your unit will be a mighty force, sir; take no prisoners."

The lieutenant had nodded, needing no clarification, and when his men drew their rations for the patrol into North Carolina they also drew double the normal issue of ammunition for the Spencers.

"We're going into the mountains and we're going to hit these ruffians with the wrath of God Almighty," the colonel had said to the departing men. Of course the colonel said 'we' when it was obvious to all that he himself was not leaving the comforts of Cleveland, but they all understood that.

And they all understood that their mission would be without any military courtesy. No white flags, no prisoners, no mercy.

***

The Foster brothers and Hattie went slowly over the lists they had recovered at the Evans Mill action. She thought often of the two Bradfords she had killed herself, the looks on their faces when her bullets had struck them.

It was as if it happened to someone else, someone far away, and she had merely been watching, or had been shown a picture afterwards. She felt no emotion when she thought of it, but she knew she should. These were the very men who had placed the noose around her father's neck, who had hanged him in Old Man Tysinger's barn. The very ones.

One had fallen in the first shots at Evans Mill and she had killed the other two. Only one had gotten away, the boy said, gone to Tennessee to join the Union Army. Maybe she'd catch him someday, too, but now three of the four guilty ones were dead and Buck Rose had been avenged. There was blood on her hands, she knew, but she did not care. It was war, like in the Bible, an eye for an eye.

She'd always liked the Bible story about David and Goliath; imagined herself as a brave David fighting the monster Union forces, winning with her wit and cunning. But she was still amazed to stop and think about where she was now, what price she was paying for warring on the Yankees.

"This is the one y'all got off one of the dead Yankees at the mill," she said, straining to see the list by the firelight in camp. Kirkwood and the others completely ignored the process, figuring that if Hattie and the Fosters came up with any new knowledge they would share it.

"Yeah, 'at there's the muster roll," the Fosters said. "Ol' Coleman Bryson wuz gonna be a captain in the Yankee army and raise hell in Murphy, wuz he?"

"Played hell hisself, ain't that right?"

"Let's go over these names one more time, I think we accounted for all these men," she said. One at a time she read off the names and they solemnly remembered each one, sometimes calling on one of the other guerillas around the fire to testify if needed.

"John Hampton."

"Shot at the mill, one of the first ones to fall."

"Ezra Tappen."

"One of the ones we shot in the woods and left."

"James Birchfield."

"I think another'n we shot in the woods, all them damn Birchfields look alike and they're all Union, but I think he's still out there in the woods."

"Harley Bradford."

"That's one of the gang that killed y'er daddy and Old Man Tysinger. Shot down in front of the mill, seen 'im myself."

"And I shot the other two Bradfords myself," she mused aloud. 'That leaves only one, a Davenport, to catch and he's somewhere in Tennessee in the Union Army."

They accounted for all they had slain that day at the mill, and later in the woods. There were six or seven names that were in doubt, men who had either not shown up for the muster or had been there and escaped in the confusion.

Hattie drew a line carefully through each name of the dead, leaving these seven (it was finally decided at seven) as the names of Union supporters still alive and kicking somewhere in the area. She folded this list and replaced it in her saddlebags.

They trusted her to do the reading, since she was the best educated of them all. The Fosters could read some, but Kirkwood and the rest were practically illiterate, able at most to write only their names.

"Now this is the list that came from Coleman Bryson's coat at his cabin. Y'all said he died trying to get to this coat so the list must have been important to him."

They nodded. The would-be Union officer had died hard, reaching for that coat. It held no weapon, nothing of importance except for a piece of paper that had names on it. She read them now.

"Tom Trull."

"Farmer over on Owl Creek. Union man, everybody knows it."

"Gene Silver."

"Damn peddler, if he's still in this country."

"Union Man."

"Might be, don't know."

"Pen Johnson."

"Any of these men at the mill?"

"Naw, n'er in the woods either."

"Then this must be a list of the next company he was gonna raise don't you guess?"

She glanced further down the list, a few of the names she recognized herself. These were not at the mill because they were being organized later.

"Hang on t'that list, girl," Kirkwood said, listening to their conversation with interest now. "It'll be good to have it. We kin look at it agin sometime in daylight. Be nice to know who was aimin' to help ol' Bryson…"

She barely heard his words, folding the paper clumsily and stuffing it into her saddlebags, hurriedly getting it away from the Fosters or anybody else who might read it.

She had just seen one name on it that caused her heart to flutter and she knew her face was flushing red in the light of the fire Maybe they wouldn't notice, she'd tell them later that she lost the list.

***

The Union patrol had eased into Cherokee County under cover of darkness, the civilian guide leading the way. His nervousness grew, the lieutenant could see that, the man was terrified of this Kirkwood.

"Where are you taking us?" he asked.

"We're going to a barn at Hanging Dog," the guide answered. "Good family, loyal to the Union, big barn. I want to keep all the men and hosses hidden out o' sight."

"Man, you don't have to be so careful," the lieutenant laughed. 'We've got fifteen men here, armed with repeaters, we can stand off an army."

"This ain't the army," the man snapped. "This, by God, is Big Tobe Kirkwood and he's got half the county er more a-backin' him. If we don't watch out, he'll know about you'uns bein' here before we're ready."

"Lead on," the lieutenant said, tiring of the lecture.

"He ain't got them fancy repeaters, but his boys is sneaky and they kin shore shoot. An' they don't call 'em bushwhackers f'er nuthin'."

They rode on in silence, guided by the civilian's light-colored horse, and reached the large barn on Hanging Dog Creek about midnight. Other than a few dogs barking, their arrival made little commotion.

A lantern lit up the interior of the barn and the weary Yankee troopers unsaddled their mounts, put them in stables and climbed into the hayloft to bed down.

***

The next morning the family from the house brought fried eggs and ham to the Yankee soldiers hidden in the barn and the pattern was repeated at each meal. The men were able to walk around and stretch their legs in the pasture, but the lieutenant kept men and horses hidden at the guide's request.

"The Home Guard at Murphy has got a sort of commisary set up in the county jail," the guide said. "They got powder and lead there an' some blankets and stuff. They take it from Union people and give it to Secesh. Sometimes the reg'lar Reb army sends patrols in here an' they help them. I want you'uns to hit it."

"How much resistance will we get from the Home Guard?"

"Not much, they're all old men and boys, nothin' but one-shot muzzle-loaders an' they'll run from this bunch with the repeaters. They killed our Sher'ff and his two boys, which wuz good Union people, and I want to see 'em hit."

In wartime, in a close-knit neighborhood like Hanging Dog, the slightest change in routine was noticed.

Neighbors saw the heavy smoke rising all day from the farmhouse where food was being prepared for the visiting Union troops. Suspicions were further aroused as daylight riders visited that farm at more than the normal rate, bringing intelligence to the guide, who relayed it to the lieutenant. Cousins of some of the spies, the cousins being Confederate sympathizers, spilled the beans to Old Molly and, through her, the Home Guard knew.

"This boy-dog is mean as hell, honey, watch this," Kirkwood said. He was training the red bulldogs to bite at a stick held by one of his men. "Sic it boy, bite it."

The red bulldogs they had gotten in Tennessee were pretty to look at and might save the camp from being surprised, Hattie thought. She liked the dramatic entrances they sometimes made, with the red dogs in front, then Kirkwood on his red horse with his red hair showing.

The female bulldog was not as aggressive as the male. She rubbed against Hattie's legs and begged to be petted. The male, however, was soon slobbering and grunting with exertion, attacking the stick again and again.

***

Old Molly herself rode into the camp, accompanied by Greybeard. Molly was riding an old mule and plainly agitated. She had never visited the camp, although it was only a mile or so out of Murphy. She had always preferred to talk to Hattie on Saturdays in town.

"Honey, help me get down."

"Moll', what in the world brings ya' out here," Kirkwood said, reaching up to help the plump woman off the mule.

"Big news, son, bad news maybe."

They chased the other bushwhackers away then and Molly spoke only to Tobe and Hattie, saying she trusted only them, some of the others might not be true.

"Been hiding in a barn on Hanging Dog. Got fifteen men, all with them repeater guns, ever' blesset one. Shoot fast as they can throw the levers on 'em, cut ya' down like a swing-blade cuts grass."

"Spencers," Kirkwood said, biting his lower lip in full concentration. "We need them guns."

"Gonna hit the commissary t'morrow mornin', darin' you er th' Home Guards to stop 'em if ya' want t' face them repeaters," she rushed on, paying no attention to Kirkwood. "Stayin' with some o' them copperheads on Hangin' Dog, hidin' in a barn," she spat. "Ain't foolin' nobody, we knowed about it the day they come here."

"Hold on a minute, Moll'," Kirkwood said. "Answer me a question. They plan to hit the jail in Murphy tomorrow?"

"Yeah, in the morning."

"Then what?"

"Goin' right back to Hangin' Dog, I think. Folks I been talkin to seem to think they may stay out there one more night and then ride 'cross the mountains to Tellico, then circle back to Cleveland."

"They ask 'bout us?"

"Yeah, ever'where. The'r here becuz o' what you'uns done t' Bryson. Th'ain't skeered o' th' Guard, but they are skeered a little o' you two."

Hattie and Kirkwood smiled at each other, hearing this. She nodded politely at Molly. Kirkwood gave the rebel yell, throwing his head back, tossing that long red hair and crowing like a rooster.

"They better be skeered," he vowed. "We'll make

'em dance before it's over."

***

The streets of Murphy were deserted the next morning when the Union troops rode in, and so was the commissary. It had, of course, been stripped of all goods and was standing open and bare.

"It looks like the enemy spies work well," the lieutenant said drily to the guide. "We won't capture much contraband here today."

"We got 'em on the run, Lieutenant," the other said, ignoring the remark. "Oh, this is a happy day f'er me. Murphy-town can, by God, kiss my ass. These Rebs have run off like skeered haints, yellow dogs, 'fraid to fight."

They rode around through the little town and were watched closely from behind curtained windows.

"Maybe we should burn their jail, force them to find a new commissary," the lieutenant mused aloud.

"Naw, don't do that," the guide said, reason returning. "We need a jail and, besides, we'll vote in another good Union man when this war's over and he'll need a place. Don't burn it."

"Where's the Kirkwood camp?"

"They say it's about two miles out of town, but I don't know 'zackly which direction, over t'ward Georgie, I think."

"Maybe we ought to ride out and hit his camp."

"If y'r plannin' that, we need to strike right at first light. R'at now wouldn't be no good, they know wh'r we're at, they'd all be gone just like at the commissary."

The lieutenant nodded in understanding, it was frustrating to try to catch enemies who fled.

"They say he's got his Indians out f'er guards," the

guide offered. "An' he's got two mean bulldogs, red as his hair, to guard the camp too. In daylight like now we'd never get anywhere close b'fore they knowed it."

"Well, let's go back to the barn. We'll start earlier tomorrow for this Tellico place, maybe catch some Rebs in the open."

***

Kirkwood had planned the ambush well. He and his men watched from a nearby ridge as the Yankee patrol rode up the Hanging Dog road toward Murphy that morning. Winds of autumn had stripped the trees of most leaves and they could plainly see the federals a half-mile away, the sun making their blue uniforms bright against the drab landscape.

"Ain't that a purty sight," he said. "Ridin' over to Murphy to whup the Home Guard. Which they're gonna find ain't at home, so they'll come r'at back up this road agin this afternoon."

When the patrol was out of sight, Kirkwood and his best shots moved into position. Hattie stayed with the horses, out of sight and well back from the ambush site, lest the horses whinny at the scent of the Yankee mounts.

"I'm takin' this bulldog, Petey, with us, boys," Kirkwood said. "It's time he tasted some Yankee blood." The dogs stayed in camp most of the time, but the male showed such a fighting streak that Kirkwood now kept the animal at his side. It growled at the other men, who were not comfortable around the beast.

At a certain point on the road, nearly halfway between Murphy and Hanging Dog, there was a red-clay bank which extended for about a hundred yards or more beside the road. It was ten feet or more above the road surface to the top of the bank and the top itself was level more-or-less, although covered in bushes. It was sort of a natural bench, the land sloping sharply up behind it into the steeper mountains.

Kirkwood and a dozen men now climbed into these bushes atop the bank, paralleling the road. The road ran uphill at this point so the Yankee horses would be straining slightly.

"This is the plan," he said quietly. "G'ither roun' an' listen good."

Like the Evans Mill ambush, the shooters were carrying two or three rifles apiece, all single-shot muzzleloaders. They could fire one, drop it, grab another and fire it, even a third if they had it. Then it would be over, or at least time for close-range knife and pistol work.

They spread out up and down the top of the bank until they were spaced out evenly along the hundred-yard firing line. Kirkwood would be at the highest point, the Foster boys would be at the low end.

"The Yanks will be strung out in a line, maybe two-by-two, maybe single file. The road's narrer here, I'magine they'll mostly be single file," Kirkwood said.

"The deal is to hit 'em hard 'fore they know what's goin' on, an' hit'll be all over with. If ya' miss a few and they get them repeaters goin', it'll shore be hard on us, drop back and run.

"Watch close on them Foster boys. When they stand up, that'll be our signal. Don't shoot 'til ya' see them Fosters stand up, got it?"

The plan was simple and lethal. The last man in the Yankee patrol would ride unknowingly past the Fosters, which would mean the entire patrol strung up the road was already in the sights of the hidden Kirkwood marksmen.

They waited, and waited. The cold December sun offered a little warmth and the red bulldog became restless. Kirkwood patted the animal and rubbed its ears. Finally they heard hoof-beats in the distance.

"I don't believe there are any Rebs around here," one of the troopers said loudly as they passed the Foster boys. "We'll be back in camp at Cleveland before Christmas."

The red-clay bank was soft and every rain washed more of it down onto the road, making it narrower. Sure enough, the Yankees were in single file, except where they rode side-by-side in conversation. The last man passed the Fosters and plainly saw them stand up with their rifles. He shouted, but it was too late.

The entire top of the bank exploded in sheets of gunfire and powder smoke. The horses screamed in terror and wounded men grunted in pain, lurching and toppling to the ground.

Shoot for the bodies, Kirkwood had told them, and they did. The Union saddles were cleared in that first awful volley and then the savage bushwhackers plunged down the bank, catching the horses and knifing the wounded.

"Easy with them knives," Kirkwood roared. "I want t'save some uniforms off 'em. Shoot 'em in the head like I do." For example, he fired his pistol point-blank into the face of the already-dead lieutenant. "Might need some blue uniforms one day, go easy on th'r shirts."

The guide, shot from his saddle by Kirkwood himself, was alive and on his hands and knees on the roadway, stunned and blood streaming from his mouth. One of the guerillas recognized the traitor and ran over to kick and curse him.

"Wait a minute," Kirkwood ordered. "Let m'dog Petey chaw on 'im a little. Sic 'im, Petey."

The bulldog attacked the wounded guide with growling and plunging, biting at the man's defenseless head and throat. Finally the animal seized the man's throat in a death-grip, growling low in its body and refusing to turn loose. It tried to shake its head from side to side, but its jaws remained firmly clamped on the guide's throat. Dying, lying on his back in the bloody road, the guide feebly tried to push the dog away.

"Ain't that a purty picture?" Kirkwood said. "Ol' Petey got hisself a copperhead, got 'im down and eatin' on 'im."

Hattie rode up then with their horses, looking down in disgust.

"Shoot the man, Tobe," she said firmly. "Put him out of his misery. Don't let the dog bite him anymore."

The Fosters had each taken a Spencer from the dead troopers' horses and one of them now put the muzzle of his Yankee rifle to the guide's head and pulled the trigger. The body convulsed once and was dead. The bulldog released its grip and walked away, licking the blood from its front paws.

"Come'ere, boy, ya' done good," Kirkwood said to it, patting the dog's head and glaring at Hattie and the Fosters. "You'uns messed up a good party."

He was mad at her, she could tell it, over the incident, and things did not get better in the days following. They had stripped several of the Union soldiers of their clothing and took all their gear and horses, leaving the bodies in the road for the Union families to dispose of. "'Er let the buzzards eat 'em."

Back in camp, they quarreled over the surplus horses and the new Spencer rifles.

"We ought to turn over these good horses to the regl'r Confederate cavalry," she said openly. "They need better mounts and we've got enough horses." He shook his head.

"C'mon, Tobe, let's give these horses for the South to use. We are supposed to be fighting for the South."

"Gonna send 'em to Knoxville and sell 'em back to the Union," he said. "We'll share the damn money."

"That's not right, Tobe."

"I'll do, by God, what I want to, girl," he swore, anger rising in his face. "An' I want something right now. Drop y're drawers."

Her face flushed at the demand for sex, right here in daylight, in front of the men. She was being intimidated by Kirkwood and he might even kill her if she refused.

"Wait 'til tonight," she said weakly, so low she could barely hear herself. "Wait 'til tonight, Tobe."

"I ain't waitin' a bit, girl, I want it now," he said and seized her and threw her roughly on the blankets they shared. She slid into the blankets and covered herself so the men could not see.

Grinning with lust and power, Kirkwood slid into the blankets beside her, fumbling with his pants. The Fosters and some of the others walked away, but some stayed to watch the activity going on under the blankets on the ground.

Hattie closed her eyes and reached around him with both arms, keeping the blankets over them. He mounted her quickly and finished just as quickly, laughing and grunting. She endured him.

"That's just to let ya' know who's boss," he said,

getting his pants back on. "Ya' don't talk back to the boss. Ya' never shoulda stopped my Petey-dog from eatin' that Yankee back there, made me look bad."

She said nothing, but glared at him, glad the near-rape was over and he had not struck her. The Foster boys tried to console her.

"That's just his way, Hattie, he really likes ya'."

She was heartened by their feelings, but did not show it, did not cry and did not speak to Kirkwood for two days. A cold rain began to fall and they tried to make a shelter from oilcloths and tree-bark.

"If we're going to stay out here in these woods all winter, we ought to get us a better camp, move into a barn or an old house," she said aloud one day, speaking to no one in particular. 'It would be a whole lot warmer."

Kirkwood said nothing; knew the wisdom of her remarks, and the underlying nagging that she was doing, aimed at him, pushing for a better place to stay. He resented that too, the womanly way of nagging at a man. He'd show her on the horses, though, he'd already sent ten of the best with four good men across the mountains to Knoxville. They'd be back in a few days with the money, most of which he'd keep for himself. Meanwhile they were eating good, well-mounted and half the men had Spencer repeating rifles. They feared nobody.

"I'm going back home for a few days," she announced. "It's Christmas next week and I want to see my brother and my Granny."

"Y'ain't mad at me, are ya', honey?" Kirkwood smiled, the threat in his gravelly voice. "Don't be mad. Ya' be sure to come back to us 'er I'll come and get ya'."

"I'll be back in a few days," she said firmly. "Don't worry about that."

She rode slowly back to her home place, first back to Murphy and then up the river to the little house where Granny and Little Buck would be waiting.

I could stay at home now with Granny, she thought, *I found the devils that killed my Papa and I got even with them. Or I could go back to Tobe and the boys and keep after these hateful Yankees.*

There was an important question to ask a certain youngster, it had lain on her mind for days now, but in the excitement of ambushing the Yankee patrol, and then the confrontation with Tobe, she had been able to put it out of her mind.

She meant to ask it, too.

What was his name doing on the secret list of Coleman Bryson supporters, the smudged pencil-written names in the coat that he had died trying to reach, the name of Little Buck Rose?

Chapter Six

Granny watched through the window as Little Buck and the Gardiner boy split wood for the fireplace, using a wedge and maul to reduce the oak chunks into smaller pieces.

Little Buck was only fourteen, but he was big for his age, she thought and a good worker. She was suspicious of the Gardiner boy's politics, but he had never said anything openly and although she had deliberately tried to eavesdrop on them several times, she had heard nothing to confirm his family's Yankee leanings.

The Gardiner boy and Little Buck had found the old dead oak on the ground, fallen to earth after a big storm a month ago. With his father's saw, Little Buck and the other boy had been able to cut the log into chunks and had hauled them to the house on a boy-drawn sled. The laborious splitting had started then.

To repay the Gardiner boy for his help, Little Buck had occasionally gone to the Gardiner place on Brasstown to do chores there. She knew it and was uneasy about his exposure to the family there, but could do nothing about it and really had no proof they were trying to turn him to the Union, except for the things that her friend Molly told her on Saturdays.

"I wouldn't trust them Gardiners," Molly said, spitting tobacco juice expertly at a rat under a wagon, "any more than I'd trust that rat there. Two o' that boy's uncles are away in the Yankee army and another'un layin' out in the woods som'ers, a-dodgin' Kirkwood."

"Moll' , I never heered th' boy say anything bad."

"Shucks, his own mama was down here last week on market day and tol' somebody that Lincoln was a good man, they tol' me bout it later, after she left. Imagine that, goin' t'town t' say things like that. An' him the biggest Yankee of 'em all, that damn Lincoln."

Granny had just shaken her head at that and stopped speaking. Her own grandson, with both his parents dead and gone, consorting with a known Union-loving family.

The War did strange things to people, she thought, *strange things.*

***

Little Buck held the iron wedge straight up in the center of the oak-chunk. The Gardiner boy, older and stronger, held the wooden maul in his hands, poised to strike. A wooden club made of extra-hard persimmon, it came down quickly on the wedge, driving it deep into the oak and opening up a large crack in the chunk.

"Here, let me try the edge of it with the axe," Little Buck said picking up his daddy's double-bitted axe and swinging it downward like a man. Careful not to hit the iron wedge, he sent the axe-blade deeply into the remnants of wood holding the chunk together and it fell into two halves, freeing the wedge so the process could start over again.

"Let's rest a minute," the Gardiner boy said, sitting down on a piece of wood. "I got something to tell ya' and we need to make plans."

Little Buck put the axe aside and listened attentively. He now trusted his older companion and was excited at the prospects of what might lay ahead of them.

"My uncle is gonna take a bunch of us to the Army headquarters at Cleveland next week," blurted the Gardiner boy."We're gonna join the Union Army. You wanna go with us?"

Little Buck thought for a long time and began to nod, lightly chewing at his lower lip in concentration. They had talked and planned of being drummer boys and fighting Indians and now it was here, his chance to get away from Granny and this war and everything else.

"The War's gonna be over anytime now," the other reassured him. 'The South's whipped, it can't last any longer. The Union is going good, we can be in their army and go out West and fight Indians. You're old enough to be a drummer boy, I might be able to be a real soldier."

"I bet they have lots to eat," Little Buck said. "I'm tired o'rabbit and groundhog, I'd like to eat pig-meat 'til I 'bout busted." The other laughed and clapped Little Buck on the back.

"You already sound like a soldier, talking 'bout grub," he said. "Now don't tell nobody and I'll tell ya' what day. It'll be next week, f'er sure. Who's that ridin' up yonder?"

"Looks like my sister," Little Buck said glumly. "Reckon she musta come home from Kirkwood f'er Christmas."

***

The day after Hattie left, the horse-sellers returned to camp with $2,000 in cash, gold money from the Knoxville quartermasters. Kirkwood rubbed his hands with glee as they poured out the gold on a flat rock and counted it in the firelight as best they could. It was difficult to count, since Kirkwood whisked away several bags of gold before they could really see it, but it seemed to be a large sum of money.

"Boys, were they picky?"

"Naw, they never asked no questions. Ya' could tell they wuz wonderin', but they wanted them hosses real bad."

"We killed the Yanks and sold th'r damn hosses back to 'em," Tobe crowed. "An' got a wagon-load o' Spencer rifles in the deal."

They laughed and patted each other on the back and even took a drink or two. Most of the time Kirkwood forbid whiskey in his camp and his rule was iron, but they had persuaded him that it was, after all, Christmas of 1864 and they deserved a little joy on the holiday.

"Pour me a l'il horn o' that ol' tanglefoot stuff," one laughed, holding his cup under the keg of whiskey. "I'll need some in me t'keep off th' cold t'night."

Kirkwood had them practice with the Spencers, teaching each other to load and shoot the repeaters. "Make sure ya' know the sights on 'em, how they're shootin', 'cause after Christmas we're a-goin' raidin' agin in Tennessee."

He gave each of them some money, keeping most of it hidden away, and sent them with two extra horses to be given to the Home Guard in Murphy, in exchange for some powder for the cap-and-ball pistols.

"We got thirty-one men in all," the Fosters reported to him. "Half of us got repeaters and we got plenty o' powder now fer the reg'lar muskets and the pistols. We're ready f'er anything."

They had given Old Molly some gold money, too,

on the trip to Murphy to trade the horses for powder, and she had sent out a cured ham, a real oddity during the War, to Kirkwood for the holidays.

"Some of you'uns wanna go home f'er Christmas, I kin understand that," he said. "Go on home and be sure to be back in a few days. Me and some others gonna stay here in camp and eat this ham. Be sure ya' leave all the repeaters here with us, we'll guard 'em. Don't want to take a chance on losin' any of 'em so don't take none home."

They dutifully obeyed, stacking the Spencers in a pyramid, counting them and covering them with two layers of oilcloth against the weather.

"Don't eat too much f'er Christmas," Kirkwood hollered as they rode out. "Don't git too fat 'er ya' cain't ride good. We'll be a-headin' out in a day 'er two when ya' git back."

He had given the Fosters a special assignment. They carried a sack full of Union uniform shirts, taken from the patrol they had bushwhacked on Hanging Dog road.

"Git y'r womenfolk to wash 'em and clean the blood out of 'em best they can," he ordered. "Bring 'em back clean an' ready t' wear. Sew up th' bullet holes and knife rips in 'em, if y'r womenfolks can do that. We just may need some blue uniforms along the way," he told the Fosters. "Might come in real handy."

***

"Oh girl, y've come home f'er Christmas," Granny gushed, glad to see her. "You kin he'p me cook, we ain't got much, but we kin shore find somethin' t'eat 'roun here."

Little Buck and the Gardiner boy glared at her and

said nothing as she dismounted.

"Buck, c'mere and give me a hug," she said. "And put up the horse for me." He complied, standing stiffly as she hugged him, the Gardiner boy watching.

"Who's that with him?" she asked moments later, inside their snug little cabin.

"One o' th' Gardiners," Granny spat in the fire. "I don't keer much f'er th'r politics, but him an' Little Buck is friends. They go to school on Saturdays t'gether in town and they hunt some and they share th'r chores. The Gardiner comes over here to h'ep Buck and Buck he goes over there to h'ep him sometimes. They 'bout got us enough wood split out f'er the rest o' th' winter."

"What about his politics?"

"Well, like I said, I don't keer much f'er that. Ol' Molly says the whole fam'ly's pure Yankee. The boy never says nothin' t' me, don't know whut he says to Buck."

They made a special trip into town since Hattie had a little money and bought some flour and meat and the two women cooked up a stew and some bread for Christmas. Little Buck ate hungrily, but said little; answering Hattie's questions about the Saturday school, but offering no additional information.

The day after Christmas, she cornered him in the barn, feeding the horse. She had burned Bryson's list, if anyone ever asked she would say she lost it, but she wanted to know why his name was on it.

"What do you and the Gardiner boy talk about?"

"About the war and all, I guess," he said, reluctant to talk to his sister, but plainly mad, once the words started flowing. "I wish this war was over. I hate to go to town on Saturdays."

"Why? Why do you hate to go to town?"

"People talk about you," he blurted, turning to face her and she could see the fire in his eyes. "People talk about you bein' with Tobe Kirkwood and it ain't nice. Granny cussed one of 'em and they hushed, but they still talk and sometimes I know they're whisperin' behind our backs."

She flushed with shame, knowing what the talk must be. She was Kirkwood's woman, everybody knew.

"Well, I'm fighting this War too," she said. "The only way I know how. And I got them murdering Bradfords, too, I reckon you heard about that."

He nodded glumly and she pressed her question again.

"What do you and the Gardiner boy talk about? He's a Yankee, ain't he? Has he got you turned into a Yankee yet?"

Buck glared at her again and started to speak, but stopped.

"Go on," she urged. "We're brother and sister, we ain't got anybody but each other. Tell me what's on your heart."

"Don't tell Granny," he said 'but we're gonna run off and join the army over in Cleveland. Goin' with a bunch of other people."

"Join the army? The Yankee army?"

"Yeah," he said stoutly, defying her with his eyes and out-thrust chin."I wanna go out West and be a drummer boy, he'p the army fight Indians."

"But, Buck, this is the Yankee army you're talking about. The Yankees killed our papa. Did you forget that?"

"The Yankees didn't kill him, at least not the army. Them men from Shoal Creek wuz the ones that done it."

"Well, they were Yankees, too," she said. "Maybe

not in the army, but Yankees just the same. You'll be joining the same side that killed your Pa."

"I don't care. I'm tired o' the killin' around here, tired of knowin' people are talkin' about you and Kirkwood, I'm goin'."

"Who'll take care of Granny?"

"She kin take care of herself. we got her enough wood cut to last out the winter."

"When are y'all going? I want to hug you again for good-bye, I may never get to see you again."

"Next week," he said. "I think maybe the end o' next week. There's a bunch planning on going, me and Gardiner are in it and lots of old men."

"You sure are stubborn," she said, hugging his small body to her and holding him like a child. "That's pure Rose, I reckon. I wish you'd change your mind."

He shook his head against her chest, but did not try to break the hug. They stood there in the barn for a long time, two children of the War, and his boyish arms went around her waist and held on tightly.

"Don't tell Granny," he said.

She felt a tear slide down her cheek and held him tighter. It was all she knew to do.

***

A few days later she rode out to the camp. It was a cold morning, brisk and clear, only a small hint of a breeze, but January for sure. The new year, 1865, was starting off with a promise of bad weather coming. Smoke was blowing, holding near the ground, low in men's eyes. The older ones said it was a sure sign of snow coming.

She dismounted with the help of the Foster boys, who tied her horse for her, and she walked toward the fire where men jostled for space. Kirkwood, recognizing her, broke away from the crowd and came to her with a big smile. He seemed glad to see her after a week's absence.

"Gimme a hug, girl," he said. "I missed ya'."

Squeezed in his bear-hug, she smelled the woodsmoke and horse-sweat on his clothing, but was not repulsed by it, rather felt a comfortable assurance in this strong man. Cruel sometimes, he still protected her and cared for her and she felt good in his presence.

"Y're still my wife, ain't ya'?"

"Yeah, sure, Tobe. You don't have to worry about that."

He hugged her again and they walked to the fire, the men pulling back and making a space for them.

"We're a-goin' t' Tennessee agin, hit 'em hard this time, boys," he said. "Git y'er stuff t'gether, I wanna be on the trail this afternoon."

He confided in Hattie that his plans were to go first across the mountains northward toward Knoxville, then come down to the vicinity of Cleveland, visit his aunt and uncle again and then back up the Ocoee Gorge to Copperhill and thence back to Murphy. The entire raid would take at least a week, maybe longer.

She was free to go with them or to stay home, it was her choice.

"I don't like camping out in cold weather much, Tobe. I think I'll sit this one out, come back to camp when it gets a little warmer."

"Fine, girl, just fine. Speakin' o' cold weather, I'll hit a store or two and try to get us some better blankets an' coats an' stuff."

Her mind was turning with her problem, but she had no one else and he was convenient.

"Tobe, there's something I got to tell you."

"Well, let's hear it, girl."

"It's my brother, Little Buck. You remember him?"

"Yeah, I seen 'im once er twice."

"He's got in with some copperheads 'roun here and they're set on going to Cleveland next week to join the Union Army. His head's full of foolishness, says he wants to join the Army and be a drummer boy and fight Indians out West."

He pursed his lips and thought hard for a moment, his gaze lifting from her and looking at his men, busy preparing for war. The Spencers were being handed out and loaded, blanket rolls were being tied on saddles.

"Don't kill him, for God's sake, Tobe. If you run into them next week, and you well might, just scare him and run him back home. Give him a good scare."

"Aw, I won't hurt him none."

***

Little Buck Rose and the Gardiner boy were trembling with excitement. It was early in the morning and they stood at the edge of the group on the outskirts of Murphy. A man was making a speech.

"We camp tonight in a barn at Wolf Creek and go on from there."

They were only half-listening to the leader tell of the plans. It was so exciting to be going, to join the army.

"I won't never come back to Murphy," Little Buck said. "Never see this ol' place agin."

"Me, neither. I'm big f'er my age, they might let me be a reg'lar soldier."

"Not me," Little Buck said. "I wanna beat on a drum, go see the West, eat lots o' grub."

"By the third day, we ought to make Cleveland. They said we kin jine up right away," the speaker droned on. He finished shortly and they trudged west. There was a light snow on the ground, only an inch or so, but in the roadway it was churned into mud by the wagon and horse traffic that used the route even in wartime.

There were six boys and about a dozen old men, some in their sixties, in the group. All were afoot, there was not a horse in the bunch.

They segregated themselves by age and their conversations marked their interests. The old men, who outnumbered the boys, talked mostly about the army pay and maybe pensions when the War was over. The boys talked about action and glorious deeds and killing Rebs.

They all knew who Little Buck Rose was and who his father had been, but the War had split many families and, after hearing his enthusiasm for the West and fighting Indians, they accepted him.

"I wish we had a drum f'er ya' r'at now, Rose, we'd let ya' beat it while we march t' Cleveland," an old man said, clapping him on the back. The convert had been accepted and welcomed and there was true fellowship as they put miles behind them, heading west.

"We're leavin' a good trail in this snow and mud," Little Buck said to one of the old men. "Reckon the Home Guard will follow us and arrest us?"

"Naw," he laughed. "Hell, boy, the Home Guard's as old as most of us. They got no burnin' desire to git into a fight er even ride out here in the country. They'll be glad to see us go."

They slept that night in the barn of a Union family on Wolf Creek and three more old men joined the group. They next morning they walked into the Copperhill neighborhood, skirting the town and starting down a trail into the Ocoee River gorge.

"It's like a ditch, ain't it?" he said to the Gardiner boy.

"Made outta solid rock with a river runnin' in the bottom of it." The rock bluffs towering high over them, the dark timber clinging somehow to the rugged land, the gurgling river fighting its way through the boulders in the stream-bed, it was a wild scene. He felt a strangeness come over him, a sense of threat here.

***

Kirkwood had led his men across the mountains, through Tellico and easily recognized some of the same country he had been through on the disastrous Athens raid, the one that had nearly gotten him killed.

This time, however, it was different and he smiled constantly at the thoughts of Unions fleeing from him. The men were on edge; when that strange smile was on him there was hell to pay.

They had a man in their number now who was from this country and they gave him a day to find old acquaintances and spies and bring them some word of the Union families and where they might be. He was very successful and on his word they raided.

Using the fast-shooting Spencers without mercy, they hit several Union farms. Men were shot down in front of their screaming families and the bushwhackers took whatever they wanted.

"It might be a hard ol' winter, boys," Kirkwood said. "We need corn f'er the hosses, and coats and blankets f'er us, if we kin find it."

They found it, at least the corn. Hoarded by Union

families against the winter, it was found in barns and cribs and the bushwhackers piled it in stolen wagons and hauled it away, like a plague of locusts on the loyalist families.

"You've killed my man and stole all our corn," one old woman wailed at the guerillas. "What are we gonna do?"

"Tell Lincoln," Kirkwood snarled. "Maybe he'll come down here an' h'ep ye."

In a crossroads town whose name they never knew, the gang descended on a country store, looted it completely and then, at Kirkwood's suggestion, burned it to the ground. Before the flames destroyed it, they had taken another wagon-load of goods, mostly coats and blankets and some shoes.

There were four wagons now, mis-matched outfits stolen where they could find them and pulled by stolen horses. One was filled with the store goods, the other three with corn piled high.

They stole ducks and chickens where they found them on the Union farms and even two small pigs. These were put into crates and lashed to the wagons.

"By God, we'll eat good when we get home," they promised each other.

"You'uns push on with them wagons," Kirkwood told them, the marauders pausing at the lower end of the Ocoee Gorge. "Take three 'er four men t'ride with ya' f'er guards and go on up the road. Find us a good place t' camp about halfway up."

The plan would be to camp in the Gorge and go on to Copperhill the next day, from there on home to Murphy. The four wagons and their escorts rumbled away slowly up the twisting road. The afternoon was slipping away, shadows were getting longer and down in the bottom of the gorge it would soon be dark and cold this January day.

"Them wagons are slow. I'd ruther wait here and let 'em get on ahead o'us and find a camp," Kirkwood said. Remembering what Hattie had told him, he added a word of warning. "An' if ya' see anything, ride back and tell us."

They built up a fire on the spot, tied the horses and lounged around the blaze, listening to the wagons disappear up the gorge, the sound could be heard for a good distance.

"I hate ridin' on a wagon," one bushwhacker said, chuckling.

"Shore glad y'had somebody else do it, Tobe. A damn wagon'll shake y'er eyeteeth out a-bouncin' over rocks, 'specially in country like this here."

There was general agreement and more laughter. They saw themselves as bold riders, not wagoneers, as cavalry and not teamsters. One broke out a coffee-pot from a saddlebag and they gathered around the fire. The raid had yielded some real coffee and they were ready to try it. Kirkwood got the first cup and they were all enjoying the aroma and taste of the brew when they heard a horse approaching, coming down the gorge.

Several snatched up their rifles and took positions in the rocks ready for action, but the rider came right into the camp and they recognized him as one of their own.

"We run into a gang o' young boys on the road, Tobe," he said.

"They asked us if we'd seen any Union soldiers today and they said there was some more old men in their group, but they wuz back up the road. Thought you'ns ought to know about it."

Kirkwood smiled and stroked his red beard thoughtfully. The bushwhackers knew the smile and knew someone was in trouble.

"Get out some o'them Yankee shirts we took off that patrol," he said. "An' make it quick. I want five men in blue shirts to go up that road in front of us, lookin' like a Yankee patrol, step to it quick now."

***

The old men could not keep up with the young boys, who were as excited as kids on a picnic outing. Little Buck and the Gardiner boy and the rest almost ran sometimes. They had eaten their meager lunch together in the gorge and then split up into two groups, the young boys going ahead and the old men bringing up the rear.

The old man who led the band told them there was an inn of sorts, a place called the 'half-way house' that was at the lower end of the gorge. They would stop there and spend the night, then walk into Cleveland and join the army the next day. In their zeal, the young boys would reach the place first, he said, so they would wait there until the old men caught up and joined them.

"I bet them wagons we just seen was bushwhackers," the Gardiner boy said.

"They said they wuz peddlers," Little Buck replied. He winced at his companion's statement, he wished things were as they seemed and people wouldn't tell so many lies and do false things. He was a trusting lad and he liked things kept simple.

"They ain't many peddlers out and aroun' durin' the War."

"Well, they said that's what they wuz. I don't

know, maybe they tol' us the truth, maybe they lied."

The afternoon was wearing on, dark would be coming soon, and they strained to see around each corner in the rocky road if they had reached the inn yet.

"Look yonder," one yelled. "Union soldiers."

They spotted the blue shirts of the five men walking their horses slowly toward them and began to cheer, boyish yelling that sounded like they had won a game.

"Hey, we made it! Ya-a-a-y."

"Mister, we're shore glad to see y'all."

"We seen some funny-lookin' wagons on th' road just back a ways. Wuz that bushwhackers? Are you'ns chasin' 'em?"

They all talked at once and several shook hands with the blue-shirted men, who assured them that the main body of the Union cavalry was right behind them and would be on the spot in a few minutes. The men dismounted and were clapping the boys on the back and shaking hands with more of them as they heard the rumble of more horses approaching, the predicted cavalry arriving.

Joy faded to terror as the Kirkwood Bushwhackers rode up, their red-headed leader laughing with murderous glee and waving a pistol as long as a boy's arm. The Gardiner youth cursed and Little Buck felt his knees begin to wobble.

They tried to run, but there was nowhere to go. The five in blue shirts on the ground had them surrounded, now pointing their pistols at the boys. Then the riders pressed in on them and they stood in a little knot, looking up at the hairy, cursing bushwhackers. Big Tobe Kirkwood was silhouetted against the darkening sky, first on one side of them and then on the other as he circled the little group of horrified boys; his hat lost in the action, the red hair and beard waving in the low sunlight. He seemed possessed by rage, and saliva plainly glistened on the beard as he ranted and raved like a madman.

"Gonna join the Yankees, were ya'? They nearly killed me on the Nottley las' year and you'ns were gonna go over to them. By God, I'll fix ya', damn pup."

With that, he pointed the big pistol into the face of the nearest boy and pulled the trigger. Two of the other boys screamed in terror and the one shot simply collapsed in a heap, his face powder-burned black and his legs kicking uncontrollably.

"God help us, the beast'll kill us all," the Gardiner boy said.

He was the tallest of the boys and now caught Kirkwood's wild-glaring eyes.

"Stand still, damn ya'," he snarled and fired point-blank into the Gardiner boy's face, but his plunging mount made aiming difficult and the slug took out the boy's right eye, but exited at an angle through the side of the eye-socket and did no other damage. The boy plunged through the circle of bushwhackers and rearing horses and ran for the river, only a few feet away.

They had been caught where a small stream emptied into the Ocoee River and he simply dove headfirst into the gurgling, rushing river. Bullets struck all around him and two hit him in the legs, but the Gardiner boy swam furiously into the whitewater, feeling the current grab him and wash him into the rapids. On the bank several of the bushwhackers fired their rifles at him, making the water dance all around his bobbing head. Soon he disappeared in the waves and rocks and they gave up.

"To hell with him," Kirkwood cursed. "The little

sonuvabitch is either dead 'er drownded. Let 'im go. Make the rest of 'em stand still."

They pressed close on the rest of the boys and Big Tobe Kirkwood shot them in the face, one by one. They cried and wet their pants and he executed them with a cold fury, saving the smallest one until last. "Ya' better not shoot that'un, Tobe. There'll be hell to pay if you shoot him."

"I know, I know, but I'll just tell'er one o' you'uns shot 'im." Little Buck Rose looked upward at the furious giant on the horse, his heart was beating so rapidly it shook his whole body. He was hypnotized by the awful carnage around him, the bodies now lodged against his shins in the dust and the mud. The horse smell and the little bubbling branch just ten feet away were present in his senses, but his eyes were locked on the shiny gaze of the man on the red horse towering over him.

Big Tobe Kirkwood laughed to himself and thumb-cocked the long-barreled revolver for the last shot. Little Buck's pulse pounded his ears and seemed like a roaring wind, his mind flashed with the picture of his dead father and of a big Indian in a feather headdress somewhere on the grassy plains.

The man brought the pistol down until the muzzle almost touched the boy's nose and fired it, right into the center of the frightened freckled face.

Chapter Seven

The Gardiner boy had been washed by the current into a still pool behind some boulders, hidden from view from the shooters on the opposite side of the river. He had feebly crawled up on the sandy bank and lain there, his lower legs still in the water, until he heard the Kirkwood gang ride away.

Got to get back across the river, he thought, *maybe I kin help Buck or the others. Maybe somebody else still alive. Gotta cross 'fore dark, gettin' cold.*

He waded into the shallow river and struck out for the shore on the other side. It was not deep, but the current was fast and strong and it carried him downstream further than he intended. Soon he was stumbling among the loose stones and came up out of the water on the road. Looking up the road thirty yards to the massacre site, he saw a pile of dark bodies lying there and knew they would be no help to him, nor he to them.

"Oh, Buck," he moaned aloud, walking toward the bodies. "I got ya' into this and look what's happened. That devil Kirkwood."

Sloshing with each step and unaware of the growing cold, he examined each body in the dusk. It was getting darker by the minute. There were bullet holes in each face, the trademark of the red-headed butcher, no doubt who personally done the killing.

He sat down on a rock and looked at his own

wounds as best he could. His vision was limited and his head hurt, but losing his eye at this point, was mostly just an inconvenience. He could not see, his field of vision on his right side was gone so he found himself doddering his head back and forth from right to left, so the good left eye could cover the whole scene. He gingerly put his finger to his right eye at one point. There was pain then, the eyeball was obviously gone. He could not bear to touch the missing-part place again.

The wounds to his legs were minor compared to the eye, both bullets having ripped shallow grooves in his thighs, but mercifully not deep. *I was shore lucky on that*, he thought, *them bushwhackers had a hard target to hit as fast as I wuz runnin'.* They both oozed blood, but would soon scab over in the cold night air.

I'm gonna have to spend the night here with them, he thought, *in these wet clothes I may just freeze to death.* His teeth were already chattering from the cold when the idea hit him. His clothes were wet, but the dead boys were all wearing dry clothing.

He unpiled them, pulling the stiff corpses apart from where they had fallen in a tangle. Soon he had them laid out separately. Two were about his size.

Working quickly, he stripped their bodies of their clothing, even their dirty underwear. Then he skinned out of his sopping-wet clothes and put on theirs, taking a shirt from this one, a pair of pants from that one, even dry shoes and socks from his dead companions.

In their pockets, he found the makings for a fire and scrounged around in the rocks and trees of the river bank for some dead wood. "Wouldn't want to do this in warm weather," he said to himself. "Might get snake-bit if this happened in the summer. Snakes all gone in the ground now on account of cold weather, no danger at all now."

He soon had a little fire going and squeezed up close to it, to ward off the creeping cold. *Kirkwood's murdering gang might come back, but I ain't got no choice. It's build a fire or die.* He listened for hooves as long as he could, but heard none and finally fell into a deep sleep beside the bodies.

***

The river was mostly a nuisance, he thought, *that slowed commerce and progress. It divided them into two towns, Copperhill on the Tennessee side and McCaysville on the Georgia side and yet the rushing stream was probably not more than fifty yards wide. After it divided the two little towns, it plunged itself into the gorge downstream into Tennessee and beyond that, he didn't know and cared less.*

The copper ore hidden in the ground was the mainstay of the area and anyone could see a rich future for Copperhill, especially if the War would end. The Indians had found the stuff first, then the whites had come in and organized things and began mining in earnest. Wagons were too slow and the route down through the gorge to Cleveland was much too dangerous.

They needed a railroad to haul the riches out and if the War would ever end, the railroad would come quickly. Then prosperity would come in large doses to Copperhill, he was sure of it.

So sure was he that he had moved here several year ago, how many was not important anymore, and had immersed himself in the life of the community. A merchant, like his brothers in Murphy, he had opened the largest store in the area (with their assistance, of course) and presided over it daily from behind the long counter.

For the Paynes were known far and wide as shrewd merchants, not just in Murphy, and the country people and the miners all came to his store to buy. The War had about put them out of business, Clayton Payne and his brothers, but they had bought up as much stock as they could when the War started and had managed to keep their places open. Money was scarce and he had accumulated a lot of Confederate notes, which were practically worthless.

"Good mornin', Mister Payne," the toothless boatman said, grinning as he extended his hand for the fare. Nodding in greeting, Clayton Payne dropped a coin in the grimy paw.

"Looks like you are the only people making any money in this War," he said. He made the same comment at least once a day, since he lived on one side of the river and his store was on the other, the boatman brought him across each morning and returned him to the home side each evening.

"Yessir, we get by; not gittin' rich, but we get by."

The boatman's snot-nosed son, a wormy little six-year-old, cast off the tie-ropes and they began the crossing. The boy was even dirtier than the father if that was possible, Payne thought, and he carefully avoided any physical contact with either of them. Payne kept himself clean and always wore a fine suit and black bow-tie; he would no more touch either of the boatmen than he would touch a hog.

It had been raining upriver and the stream was muddy this morning, the current swift. *A bridge would be much better,* he thought, *and would come after the War.*

Public subscription would be the way, and if enough community financial support could be shown, they could issue some bonds and gather enough money to put in a good public bridge spanning the river. It would be much more convenient than the ferry these rascals ran, cheaper and much quicker, allowing for easy passage back and forth across the stream.

"I wish we had a bridge," he said. Like the remark about the money, it was a usual comment he made during crossing and the boatman endured it with patience. "We could cross day or night, high water or not, if we had a bridge."

"Yessir, I suppose so, but if you'uns put in a bridge, me an' this boy'll have to find somethin' else to do."

"That's true, it certainly is."

He absent-mindedly pulled the big gold pocketwatch from his vest pocket and checked the time. They were a little late, probably because the rising water made it slower for the boatmen, pulling on the long rope which stayed in place permanently and provided a means for getting the wooden barge back and forth across the river.

The watch and chain, with its Masonic emblem, marked him as a man of substance and he was fond of checking the time often. He had been a charter member of Cherokee Lodge #146 at Murphy along with his brothers and wore the Masonic emblem proudly.

He also carried a pistol daily, a small cap-and-ball tucked in his coat pocket. Ruffians had entered his store only once and then had backed away when they saw the gun. *Clayton Payne was not a man to be trifled with,* he told himself, *he would not stand for foolishness.*

There was talk around, always talk, about bushwhackers and guerillas who looted towns and robbed stores and people, but so far he had not seen that side of the War, and therefore doubted its severity. The social fabric had been strained, but not split yet, by the War. Up to this day, Clayton Payne had been able to intimidate his customers with his bearing and his good clothes, he was obviously a man of wealth and influence and they respected him. Even the ruffians he had thrown out of the store that day did not have the nerve to go against him and his small pistol, because he represented the establishment, the civilized part of society. He was right and they were wrong, and they had known it.

They were nearly to the bank when he heard the boatman curse.

"God-damn, looka yonder."

A staunch Baptist, Clayton Payne ordinarily did not stand for blasphemy in his presence and would have turned to give the man a good lecture, but his attention was drawn by the boatman's pointing finger. It gestured toward a group of horsemen on the road at the ferry landing, very close and looking down on them.

"It's Kirkwood f'er sure. God-damn, he don't take no prisoners."

Clayton Payne's eyes were drawn to the arrogant man in the center of the riders, his red hair and beard blowing slightly in the January breeze. It was clear but chilly and not a word was spoken by the rider now less than thirty yards above them and commanding the scene.

The boat bumped into the bank and the boy jumped to tie it. The boatman simply stood on his craft, transfixed by the murderous gang above them, simply sitting on their horses and enjoying the panic they inflicted.

No prisoners, no prisoners, the thought hammered in Clayton Payne's brain and screamed through his senses. In desperation, he drew the little pistol and waved it above his head, so the raiders would see it and perhaps be frightened of it. Maybe order could be restored by this, his symbol of authority.

Then sheer terror seized him and he ran, not well, but with spirit. He was clumsy, running sideways on the river-bank, trying to scoot around the stumps and boulders in his path and get some distance between himself and the bushwhackers. The red-headed beast, that's what his customers had called this Kirkwood, the red-headed butcher. If they stalled for long on the road above him, perhaps he might escape.

"That must be the mayor, Tobe, look at that suit on the feller. Look at that little pistol he's wavin', he might shoot us."

Much laughter and keen fascination as the big leader dismounted and snatched his own Spencer from the scabbard.

"Le's see if I kin shoot one o' these Yankee rifles, boys."

He knelt in the edge of the roadway, the horses backing away from him, and took a snap-shot at the fleeing man running to his left and now a good forty yards below him. The bullet struck well behind the running man and ricocheted with a whine into the river, sending up a spray of water.

"Hellfire, Tobe, ya' missed 'im. Try agin."

Kirkwood levered another round into the rifle and swung the barrel so the front sight passed the running man. When he judged it to be leading the target enough, he pulled the trigger.

At the sound of the shot, there was a second sound, like a stick hitting leather, a loud smack when the slug hit. The bushwhackers cheered, their horses danced away from the loud rifle and Clayton Payne staggered and fell, the heavy lead bullet having penetrated both lungs.

"Good shootin', Tobe. He's down now."

Grinning at his men, Kirkwood plunged down the bank to his trophy and approached the dying man cautiously, snatching the small pistol from the motionless hand. Then he rolled the still-conscious man on his back and stripped the gold watch from his victim.

"I'll give this gold watch and his little gun to Hattie when we get back," he said, remounting. "That'll git me back on 'er good side."

"You may have to do more'n that," they told him solemnly. "Killin' her brother wuz bad business."

"Aw to hell with 'er brother. The damn pup shoulda never tried to join the Yankees..."

They sent the wagons on to Murphy then and the riders turned south, into Fannin County, Georgia, burning a house and barn near Blue Ridge. The country was theirs.

***

The Gardiner boy woke up on the bank of the river at the lower end of the Ocoee gorge, where the Maddens Branch runs into the larger stream. The little fire had gone out in the night, but he had gotten up while it was still going and put on a second set of dry clothing from the dead boys near him, pulling their clothes on top of the first set of clothing he had taken from the bodies.

Now dressed in two layers of shirts and pants and mis-matched coats, he had survived the cold night and stiffly got up from the ground beside the cold ashes.

Stamping his feet and swinging his arms as best he could, the Gardiner boy felt his circulation surge and something akin to warmth, at least an awareness, swelled through his arms and legs.

"Well, Kirkwood, at least you'uns didn't kill me," he said loudly, feeling better at the sound of his own voice in the lonely gorge. "I'm gonna make it outta here, too."

He glanced down at his companions, especially Little Buck Rose, now stiff and dead and frozen in the road, looking like logs lying there. He had robbed the clothes off some of them, they all looked so pitiful. He turned his head, choking back the tears, and stepped boldly back toward Copperhill and Murphy.

His leg wounds throbbed now, but the thing that bothered him most was losing his right eye. He found himself constantly swiveling his head back and forth from side to side, to make up for lost vision by using the good left eye to scan his surroundings. He was completely blind on the right side and felt vulnerable, afraid he would step off the narrow road and hurt himself, or fall into an unseen hole on his right side.

Curiously, there was little pain from the terrible eye-wound, just a bad headache that would not go away. The cold night had resulted in thick scabs forming, he could feel them with his probing fingers. And he was starting to get hungry, real hungry.

He walked up the road through the gorge and the exertion warmed him. For more than an hour he walked, back toward the lone house in the middle of the gorge, where they had stopped. It had only been the day before, somehow he knew that, but it seemed like a year ago when he and the rest had stopped at that house, on their way to Cleveland. Maybe someone there could help him.

***

The next few days passed in sort of a blur for the Gardiner boy. Later he would look back and try to remember what happened and in what order it happened, but it was all fuzzy in his mind.

He had reached the house in the middle of the gorge that morning, and stumbled into the yard. People had run out to meet him, including the hysterical woman whose husband had been shot down in front of her eyes by Kirkwood. She had screamed at him, thinking somehow that he was one of Kirkwood's men, until she noticed his eye shot away. Then she had changed completely and tended to his wound as best she could.

Some of the old men from Murphy who had been with his group appeared then and asked about the other boys. He told them, in halting sentences, what had happened and felt like he was going to cry as he heard his own voice drone on with the awful story:

"Killed ever' one of 'em, 'ceptin' me. An' he 'bout killed me, too. Jumped in th' river and swum across, them dirty devils shootin' at me ever' foot o' th' way."

"We run," the old men, with a note of triumph in their voices, or at least survival. "By God, we hit the woods when we heered 'em a-comin'. They killed this woman's man and another feller that wuz stayin' here with 'em, but they never got any o' us."

The Kirkwood gang had tried to steal the horses that belonged to the house, they said, but in the confusion had only frightened the animals so bad they ran away and had now been recovered.

"It was right at dark when they hit us here," they said. "That's the only thang that saved us. They couldn't see too good 'er they'd a-rode us down. They'd caught some o'us f'er sure if it had been good daylight."

***

With the dead in a borrowed wagon and the rest walking, the sad group had made their way back to Copperhill, where a kindly old doctor dressed the Gardiner boy's wounds and they heard of the dreadful murder of Clayton Payne, a leading merchant, they said, and a fine man, but a poor runner.

They finally reached Murphy and the people gathered and moaned over the bodies of the dead boys. Even strong Southern sympathizers were shocked that Kirkwood would kill these boys. There was some surprise that Little Buck Rose, whose father had been a Home Guard, was with them and now lying here dead, but there was understanding, too. The War brought many strange things, and death was becoming far too common among them.

More than one said they wished the War was over and there was muttering that Kirkwood had gone too far this time, there was no need to kill these boys. Even Ol' Molly patted the Gardiner boy on the back and tried to hug him and everybody knew where her feelings were. He knew she was close to the Rose family.

"I got to tell Hattie," he had blurted. And she had understood and had helped him. They borrowed a buggy and went out to the Rose place, Ol' Molly went with him, and they had told Hattie June and Granny about the death of their last male.

***

The ragged riders were plainly not regular soldiers for either side, and so to be feared even more, since they apparently answered to no known authority.

After killing Clayton Payne in cold blood at Copperhill's ferry landing, the blood-lust in Big Tobe Kirkwood seemed to suddenly fall away and he ordered no more raiding for a while. He brooded and talked little but kept them riding for hours at a time, crossing through lots of mountain country.

"Whur we goin'?"

"Just to hav' a look aroun', boys, just to look."

They rode on, soon coming into little settlements where the red-headed butcher was not known and the people feared them less. The Spencers in their saddle-boots drew stares too and one rash youth in a North Georgia crossroads tried to buy a rifle off one of the gang.

"Mister, I'd shore like to have that rifle."

"What'll ye give, son?"

"I got a twenty-dollar gold piece my pappy giv' me 'fore he went off to th' War. Been savin' it f'er two years." The words just tumbled out of the youth, who had big eyes for the repeater.

"Lemme see the gold piece, we might trade," the bushwhacker said as his comrades smirked and even giggled out loud. This was too much, too easy. Even Kirkwood stopped and turned around in the saddle to see the transaction.

The youth reached into his pocket and drew out the gold piece, holding it up for the bushwhacker to see, bright yellow in his open palm. The bushwhacker reached over and took the coin, as if to examine it better and the youth gave it up.

The whole gang howled with laughter now and the bushwhacker tossed the gold coin to Kirkwood, who caught it in the air and dropped it into his coat pocket.

"Hey, gimme back my gold piece."

"Sic 'im, Petey," Kirkwood growled. The red bulldog dove at the boy and he instantly knew he had been robbed and he was now in real danger. Petey bit the youth once on the upper thigh, tearing his pants, but the boy's frantic running broke the hold and he soon jumped a picket fence into the yard of a house, the bulldog now chasing up and down the fence, looking for an opening to go through and continue the attack.

"Attaboy, Petey, bite his ass."

The bushwhackers, who disliked Petey and feared him, cheered and laughed at the sight. The dumb boy had given up his gold and the vicious bulldog who guarded their camps each night was chasing him away.

They rode away from that incident and continued south to Ballground and then south some more.

At Canton, they saw the devastation left by Sherman's troops six months previous. At least half the dwelling houses were burned to the ground, the wreckage still visible. It would be years before the town was normal again.

"It's over, it can't last any longer," an old man told them at Kennesaw. They rode back north and east and saw more destruction, more farms grown up in weeds, more hollow-eyed people weary of war and death.

It was February of 1865, the whole country seemed to be holding its breath for the war to be finished.

Somewhere east of Cumming, along the Etowah River, from a man they met on the road the bushwhackers learned of a prosperous family nearby, slaveholding farmers and loyal to the South, known to keep a stock of special chewing tobacco.

"They flavor it with rum and molasses and it's real good, I never tasted it but one time at Christmas," the man said. "It'd shore be good r'at now."

Kirkwood's mouth literally began to water. He only used tobacco occasionally, but the man's enthusiastic description had fired his senses and now he could almost taste that sweet rum-and-molasses tobacco, heavy and thick and dark. He barked out orders and soon the Fosters and one other bushwhacker, three men in all, were riding toward the big house above the river, guided by the instructions from the man they'd met.

"Get us some of that special tobacco," he told them. "Buy it if you have to, steal it, take it, whatever. Surely three men can get it so we'll wait here. If you run into trouble, we'll come and help."

The house was big, two-story, with an open porch across the front of both stories. Columns of white-painted wooden lumber supported the roof and there were brick chimneys at each end of the house. It was rather plain, not the showy mansion of a low-country plantation, but it was solid and had an air of good living about it. There was a fence surrounding the yard, which was swept clean, not a blade of grass showing.

"Looks like nobody's at home today."

"Hell, ride on in. Look sharp, we might get shot at."

One of the Fosters kicked the gate open without dismounting and then single-file, they rode their horses into the packed-clay yard, right up to the porch. It was insolent behavior among civilized people to ride inside a fenced yard, but they had been on the outlaw trail so long it mattered nothing now.

"Get them hosses outta my yard," the little woman said, in a voice firm, but not loud enough to wake the sleeping baby in her arms. She had appeared like a ghost, suddenly on the porch in front of them and not ten feet away.

"What?!"

"Y'all heard ever' word I said. Get them hosses off my yard and outside the fence."

"We just want some o' that special tobacco they say you'uns have," the Fosters said, "then we'll be on our way." They made no motion, no movement at all and sat on their mounts, looking her in the eye. From her position on the porch, she was looking at them level.

"I'm gonna shoot the first man that tries to get down off his hoss," she said quietly. They saw the pistol then, held in her right hand, coming out from under the sleeping infant and pointed right at them. The sound of the hammer being cocked could be heard plainly by all three men.

"Damn, I hate to get killed over a plug o' tobacco," the nearest Foster said. At this short range, his chances were not good and he knew it.

"Boys, she'll never get all three of us."

"I'm aimin' right at you, I'll get you first," she said, and jostled the baby over more on her left arm, so the gunhand could be raised slightly. She was standing her ground. "Now y'all get outta here."

"She means it, boys, le's go."

Sheepishly they turned their mounts and rode out of the yard, not looking back. Out of range, they discussed riding back on her with rifles blazing, but did not really want to kill a woman and baby for tobacco. It ain't worth it, they agreed, and rode back to Kirkwood for a certain tongue-lashing.

"She stood you'uns off with a pistol by herself?" he asked, laughing and shaking his head and the others joining the laughter. "Three bloody bushwhackers stood off by a woman with one pistol, and a baby in her arms?"

They grinned in embarrassment and their displeasure was even more amusing to the others, who taunted them about the incident for days. Kirkwood enjoyed it too and they rode on, not pressing their will on the local population. The gold piece they had taken from the boy went to buy corn for the horses and it was at least two weeks after the Copperhill shooting before they crossed the state line from Georgia back into North Carolina.

"Them Georgia people are tough, ain't they?" he said. "Specially the women an' children." Laughter. "We'll send the Fosters back if we hav' t' fight babies and women, won't we?"

They all agreed that the war had to be over soon, the people were tired of it. They talked of going out West when it was done, maybe sooner. Nobody would know them in the West and a man could find a living there.

"What are ya' gonna tell Hattie about her brother?" they asked.

"I'm gonna give her that fancy gold watch I took off that feller at Copperhill," he said. "An' I'm gonna tell her that I didn't shoot her l'il brother, that one o' y'all did an' I tried to stop it but you'uns wouldn't never listen."

***

Hattie sat in a big wooden rocking chair on the narrow front porch of their house and rocked, hour after hour, looking down the road and saying nothing, sometimes crying softly. Granny tried to console her, but could not seem to reach her.

The Gardiner boy had insisted on coming to tell

her personally and he looked awful, his eye shot away and scabbed over, just a raw hole in the side of his head.

"Miss Hattie," he had blubbered. "It'uz all my fault, it's my fault, all of it. I talked 'im into it."

"No," she had protested, taking the sobbing hurt boy into her arms.

They had stood there holding each other, crying in the sunlight, and he had felt her body shudder with emotion as she screamed no, no, no, again and again. In her mind she could see the twisted hateful face of Big Tobe Kirkwood and his fierce bearded riders and she focused on him, the devilish bastard.

Finally the Gardiner boy had gone away, back to his people, and she had talked some to Granny.

"I told Tobe about them going," she sobbed. "So it's my fault more than the Gardiner boy's. I told Tobe not to hurt 'em, just to scare 'em back home."

"He was not supposed to hurt them at all," she said again and again, but the reality was there and would not go away. Her little brother was dead, lying dead in a box right there in front of her, all because she had told the redheaded butcher about him, and her heart was heavy with anger and grief.

"Girl, you never even tol' me he wuz goin'," Granny said. "He'uz just a boy."

"Well, I never thought we could stop him once his mind was made up," she said. "He would go whether we liked it or not, so I was glad he at least told me about it. Then I told Tobe and I thought he'd scare all of them and they'd come running back to Murphy.

"And I wasn't sure Tobe would even see them," she added. "The day they would be coming down the road, Tobe and his men might have been off somewhere else raiding. For all I knew, he might miss them and Little Buck might end up in the Union army after all. There wasn't much I could do. And it all ended up so bad."

She rocked and cried and thought and hated and Granny forgave her on the spot for not telling about Little Buck. The old woman brought food to the girl and she ate, her feet curled up under her in the big rocker, her father's favorite chair in the whole house.

"We got to bury Little Buck, girl, get up," Granny said. Some of the Home Guard, regardless of the boy's defection, were going to help them. They had provided a coffin and they had dug the grave so the troubled boy could be buried beside his father in the Methodist cemetery in Murphy.

Hattie looked at Granny and now she seemed firm, a sense of purpose corning over her.

"Where's the clothing he was wearing when he got killed?"

"On the back porch, girl, why? I was aimin' on burning it when we git back from the buryin'."

"Gimme the scissors."

Neighbor women had come to the house and helped Granny to wash the body and change clothes on it before placing it in the coffin. Hattie had taken one terrible look at her brother, the powder-burned face and the cruel hole in the forehead and almost fainted. She had left the room then and not gone back, not even to see how he looked cleaned up and dressed in the best clothes they could find, which included a coat of her father's, too big for the boy, but the best they could do.

Now, scissors in hand, she poked quickly through the pile of bloody and dirty clothing he had worn. The shirt he wore in the Ocoee gorge was light gray in color, faded to almost white. It was now stained with his blood, a rusty brown color, and stiff to the touch. She picked it up and said, "This will do just fine, help me hold it."

Granny, shaking her head, helped the girl and they cut out a large swatch of the discolored fabric, about a square foot in size.

"I'm keeping this," she said, "to help me remember."

***

An hour later in the Methodist cemetery, on the high point overlooking Murphy, they listened to the words of an old preacher and watched the Home Guard men lower the box into a fresh hole in the ground. Hattie June did not cry and those attending the funeral watched her closely, looking at the set of her jaw and her glaring eyes, and knew the War was not over yet.

Chapter Eight

"Damn, I shore miss Hattie."

"You might miss'er a long time 'fore she comes back, Tobe," they told him. "An' she mite never come back."

He thought about that for a day or two, wandering around the camp. It was good to be back close to Murphy, the camp seemed quiet and safe. He rubbed Petey's ears and the powerful red bulldog licked his fingers. The female bulldog had disappeared sometime along the way, he didn't miss her, but he did miss Hattie June Rose.

Mostly he missed her at night, in his bed. The long ride down into Georgia and back had left him hungry for a woman, his woman, and it frustrated him. He tried to tell himself that she would forget her brother, that he would blame it on his men, but her absence showed she probably blamed him. It made him angry.

He called the Fosters to him and the three of them had a private session. There was no joking this time, he was deadly serious and they knew it.

"Y'all went to school with her, I know that, and she's known you two longer than she's known me. I want you to go to her and take this message."

They nodded solemnly and listened, he dug into the gold money he had stashed in a hollow tree near the camp and gave them a hundred dollars to split between them.

"Tell her that I never shot her brother, that somebody else in the bunch done it, you don't know who fired the shot. Tell her I want her to come back to camp. If she don't, I'll come and get her."

The Fosters were uncomfortable with the mission, and the message, but took it to Hattie a few days after Little Buck had been buried. She hid in the house when she heard hoof beats, but came out when she saw the familiar brothers.

They dismounted and sat on the edge of the porch and talked for a long time with her.

"He wants you back, Hattie."

"I'm not surprised, I sorta figured it would come to this."

"He sent us to tell ya' he never killed Little Buck."

"That's a damn lie and y'all know it," she snapped. "He's a liar and a coward to boot. How come he never came to me himself?"

"We don't know, Hattie."

"I know what for, too."

"He just wants you back in camp."

They told her of their long ride down into Georgia and what they saw, how they felt the War would be over soon. She calmed down and was kind to them, although the fire of her hatred for Kirkwood shone in her eyes.

"Hattie, he said if you don't come back, he'll come and get you."

"Come back Saturday and I'll give my answer."

They had ridden away then, satisfied with her response, and Kirkwood had grudgingly accepted it.

Some sort of plan had to be figured out, she knew that as she watched the Fosters ride off. Something had to be done, a trap to be laid, something. She had bought some time, but that was all. And she had another problem.

She had dodged it as long as she could and she turned to Granny, good ole Granny, who had suffered herself for so long and so hard, taking care of them all and now burying them all except her.

"Oh, Granny, talk to me," she said, near to tears and hating the weakness in herself. She rarely cried except in mourning. "I'm in such a mess. I hate Tobe Kirkwood -- I hate him, I hate him--and he's sent his men to get me. Said he'd come himself to take me back if I don't go back to him. I want him dead, what can I do?"

The old woman listened and looked at her granddaughter. She had seen it all and another woman's tears were just part of the passing pictures; looking back over her seventy years there had been more than a few tears, and she had gained wisdom, though few asked her for it.

"Ya' need to kill 'im, fer sure, that's a fact," she said, spitting in the fire like a man. "The rascal shot Little Buck and he orta get shot hisself. How to do it is y'er problem." She spat again. "Hit's a woman's lot to be weak, not strong like a man. But, girl, in lots o' ways a woman's shore smarter'n a man. You think about that some. On account o' her bein' weak, a woman has to use her head. A man don't think like a woman cuz he don't have to. If he wants somethin' heavy moved, why he jus' picks it up and moves it. If a woman wants somethin' heavy moved, she has to think about it a lot, figure out the easiest way t' move it her-ownself 'er better yet, talk some boy 'er man into movin' it fer her. See what I mean?"

Hattie nodded and listened and thought about her other problem.

"A man kin fight, he's strong and quick and maybe a little dumb. A woman kin nag a man into fightin' fer her. She kin persuade a man to do somethin', but she cain't make 'im do it 'cause he kin whup her if he wants to. She kin whup a little child and force it to do things, but a man'll whup her if she gets on the wrong side of him. Understand?"

Hattie was hearing and thinking. She was going to have to tell Granny, there was no way around it.

"Ya' want Tobe dead. I agree with ya'. It's the only decent thang to do, considerin' what he's done to us, but ya' can't do it yerself. He'll kill ya' girl, if he even thinks y'er a danger to 'im. Ya' need help."

Hattie felt the tears flow down her cheeks and her words tumbled out like water, she had to tell somebody.

"Granny, I feel funny inside and I know what it is. I hate Tobe and I want to kill him, but I've got his baby inside me."

***

Doyle Birchfield was a careful and a cautious man, stingy with his money and his efforts. They described him as being tight as the bark on a tree and they said he would skin out a piss-ant for its hide and tallow if the circumstances demanded it.

Now he stopped his horse in the edge of the woods and sat there watching the house, picking his teeth with a splinter and turning it over in his mind again. Was it an ambush or was it real?

He chewed thoughtfully on the splinter and nudged the horse with his boot-toes, starting it down out of the timber and into the open. As far as he knew, only two women were in that house, the home of the late Buck Rose, Confederate supporter and Home Guard. He sure felt strange riding into an enemy home, but the girl was supposedly there, the lover of that devil Tobe Kirkwood. Said she wanted to see him, Doyle Birchfield, a staunch Union man rarely seen by anyone. Mostly he lay out in the woods, trying to survive this stupid war. She had sent the message through the Gardiners.

His own brother had been killed by the Kirkwood Bushwhackers at Evans Mill, trying to join up with the Bryson company, and so Doyle Birchfield was leery of Hattie June Rose, for good reason. The reward was the only thing that really brought him here and he knew it.

Just last week he had been in contact with regular Federal cavalry, stationed now at Copperhill in a new camp there. The Yankees were offering a $5,000 reward in gold money for Kirkwood, dead or alive, for all their men he had killed plus all the loyal Union families he had raided.

Few people knew of the reward money, posters had not gone up in the towns yet, and Doyle Birchfield was a man who could use a fortune in gold. Maybe she could help him get it.

They say Kirkwood killed her little brother, he thought to himself, *that's the ticket. She may be mad enough to help us get him, to pay him back for shooting her little brother. That money could be all mine, real soon.*

Surely they wouldn't go to this much trouble just to bushwhack me, just one man, he thought. *Surely they ain't got men inside that cabin with them rifles ready to shoot me down.*

Gingerly, he guided the horse into the yard and let it walk slowly up to the door, ready to spur it into escape if anything looked wrong. It was early in the morning, he could smell their cooking smoke and the scent of meat frying.

Suddenly the door flew open and there stood Hattie June Rose, fire in her eyes and a Spencer carbine leveled in her hands, pointing right at him.

"You Doyle Birchfield?"

They stared at each other for a long minute, the Union man and the young woman who belonged to the red-headed beast. She had the drop on him and they both knew it, but apparently she meant him no harm.

"Put your horse in our barn so nobody can see it from the road. Then come on in and eat breakfast with us."

Knowing he was in the stronghold of the foe, he felt strange, but Doyle Birchfield ate with the two women and enjoyed the meal. They had ham and cornmeal mush and it was good. They smiled at his appetite, watching him wolf down his food.

"I want Tobe Kirkwood dead," she told him. "I want to see him dead more than anything and I want you to bring Yankee soldiers down on him to get the job done."

"Ya' plannin' on hittin' the main camp?"

"No, no, just Kirkwood. The rest of 'em don't bother me. I'll fix it so he'll be alone and that's when they can get him."

He could tell by the emotion in her voice, so cold for one so young, that she indeed meant to betray her guerilla lover and this was a pressing need with her, she would be laying her own life on the line to see it done.

Her plan was simple and deadly, he could see that she had made ambush plans before and had learned well from Kirkwood. *The girl was real,* he thought, *like being in the presence of a rattlesnake, full of death and cold in-*

tent. He saw no reason to mention the reward.

"There is an old house at the head of the Killian branch," she told him, "about three miles out of Murphy. The people who live there all died out, from a fever of some sort, and nobody wants to live in the house anymore because they're scared of the fever. Tobe's back in camp and he's sent for me. I'm planning on meeting him alone, it'll be just me and him, at that old house on Sunday for dinner. That's when he can be taken."

He nodded and chewed on the inside of his lip, thinking of her plan, how well laid it was, and he thought of the weight of $5,000 in gold coin, how it would feel in his hands.

"How about you?" he had asked. "He may shoot you when the soldiers come."

She grinned and shook her head. "Don't worry about me, I'll run or jump out a window or something. Where are your soldiers, in Cleveland?"

"No," he said, "a squad of Yankee soldiers now camped near Copperhill and I'll take the message to them this very day. They would be glad to capture or kill Big Tobe Kirkwood."

"One other thing," she told him, "and this is the most important of all. I want you to leave a rag on a bush in the yard of the house, that'll be a signal to me that soldiers are there in the woods around the house and everything is ready. If I don't see a rag, I'll know the soldiers are not coming and I may run myself before Tobe gets there. No rag, no deal."

He nodded again, this girl was awesome, nothing left to chance. Late that afternoon he rode into the new Union camp at Copperhill and asked to speak to the captain. He had been at the camp the week before and the pickets recognized him as a loyalist.

"I got th' big boy f'er ya'," he blurted to the officer, grinning and slapping the man on the back in his glee. The dollars fairly danced in his eyes and the show of emotion was rare for Birchfield, who was conservative in everything, even joy or sorrow, but the beauty of her plan, the gold reward almost in reach, he could not contain himself.

"What the devil are you speaking of?" said the captain, shrinking away from the back-slapping. He was not accustomed to such familiarity from roughly-dressed mountaineers, even if they were loyal to the Union.

"I kin deliver Big Tobe Kirkwood to ya', on Sunday in Murphy."

***

Kirkwood was getting jumpy now, this waiting on Hattie made him nervous, he purely hated to wait on anything. With a jerk of his head, he motioned the Fosters to come to him.

"It's Saturday mornin'," he snarled. "Go talk to Hattie agin f'er me, she said she'd have an answer today. Tell'er if she ain't comin', I'll be comin' out there to get 'er."

The two brothers rode to Murphy from the camp and then up the river road to the little Rose place. Hattie met them at the door and invited them in.

"I've decided to go back to Tobe," she said. "Y'all can tell him that. There's an old house at the head of the Killian Branch, not far from town. Nobody lives there." They nodded, they knew its location. "I want to meet him there tomorrow for a fine Sunday dinner, just me and him. Nobody else, tell him that, I want it to be just us. We got some talking to do and after that, we can come back to camp."

They looked at her intently, she seemed genuine and they had known her for years.

"Granny's got two chickens in a coop out back. We're gonna kill one and fry it up real nice. I'll have fried chicken for Tobe and fresh cornbread, it'll be a regular picnic. Y'all can tell him that. Here, I'll even write him a note you can take. Y'all might have to read it to him though, I don't think he can read very well."

She hastily scribbled out a note on a piece of paper and handed it to the older Foster brother, who folded it and put it in his pocket "Tell him to get there about dinnertime, around the middle of the day," she said. "And this is real important. I know how nervous he is about things. If everything is all right, I'll put a rag on a bush in the yard 'cause I'll get there first and have the food and all ready for him. If he sees the rag on the bush, fine, if he doesn't, tell him to turn around and ride off. I'll hide my horse out behind the house so the rag'll be the only signal."

The Fosters took the message back to camp and Kirkwood was standing there waiting for them, hands on his hips.

"What did she say?"

"Looks like y're forgiven, Tobe," the eldest Foster said, grinning as he handed Kirkwood the note. "Y're invited to a picnic tomorrow, with fried chicken and a purty gal and a big house with nobody else around."

They told him about the arrangements and to look for a rag on a bush in the yard, that would be Hattie's all-clear signal. He nodded, listening, he liked that. And he turned the note over and over again, looking at it.

"Read it to me, boys, I ain't got my glasses with me," he said.

They had never seen him read anything before, with glasses or without, but said nothing and took the note back. The elder Foster read from the note to him:

Dear Tobe,

You are invited to a picnic dinner on Sunday at noon at the old house on the Killian Branch. Please come alone as we have lots to talk over. After all, we are old married people (ha-ha) and we can ride back to camp when we are done talking.

Love, Hattie

He made them read it over to him three times, listening close to each word and each phrase, trying to sift out the true meaning.

"Reckon she means it, she's gonna come back all right?"

"Yeah, Tobe, we talked to her at her house a long time and then she sent ya' the note. She seems over it and ya' know, ya' helped 'er git them Bradfords that killed her poppa. She knows that and you kin remind'er of it if ya' need to. We think everything's gonna be fine."

***

At the Rose farm, Hattie had cut off the head of a chicken with her father's axe and the bird flopped around, slinging blood until it died. Then she and Granny had boiled a pot of water and put the scalding water on the bird to loosen the feathers, then it had to be picked clean and cut into frying-sized pieces.

"We'll get up real early t'morrow morning' to fry it up nice and brown," Granny said. "What are ya' doin' with that rope?"

Hattie had located a piece of plowline in the barn and brought it into the house.

"Granny," she said, and a smile crept over her face. "Can you help me tie a hangman's noose in this rope?"

***

In the guerilla camp, Sunday morning dawned bright and clear, none of the early-morning fog which often wraps the mountains. It was the first day of March, 1865, although none of the bushwhackers had a calendar, they had only the most vague notion of the passage of time.

Their numbers fluctuated from time to time and now were down to less than 20 men, a large number of the riders having gone home or drifted elsewhere. The end of the War had to be coming soon, they could all feel it.

"You stay here, Petey, y'ain't goin'," Big Tobe Kirkwood growled at his dog. "I'm making' a social call on Hattie June and I don't need no dogs around."

There had been much joking as he prepared for the promised Sunday picnic, bathing in the little stream that ran near the camp and even shaving some of his scraggly red whiskers off.

"Boy, ya' shore look purty, Tobe, ya' mite not get past Murphy. One o' them town women mite jump out an' grab ya'."

Kirkwood grinned and put on his best boots, stolen off a dead Yankee officer, and adjusted his slouch hat. Even on a social call, he went heavily armed. Two pistols under the big coat, the Spencer carbine in the scabbard and a double-barreled shotgun he had begun carrying in recent days, the barrels sawed off to a shorter length for quick action.

"Hell, ya' got enough guns to stand off an army, Tobe."

"Just goin' t'bring my wife back, boys, a man can't be too keerful."

"Yer wife? I heered that all right." More laughter.

He mounted the big red horse and rode slowly out of camp. He knew where the house was; they had drawn him a map of it, easy to find, told him to look for the rag on the bush, said Hattie's horse would be hidden out back, but she would put a rag on a bush if everything was safe for him to ride in.

Not long after Kirkwood rode out of camp, a guerilla who had ridden with them in the past came in and spoke briefly with the Fosters and then rode away again. He came from the lower end of the county and brought them the first word of the reward on Kirkwood.

"A price of $5,000 in gold for Tobe Kirkwood? That's a lot o' money."

"Reckon we ought to ride out after him and tell him?"

"Naw, we kin wait till him an' Hattie gets back, tell 'em both then. They'll know what to do."

***

In the woods near the old house, the Union captain and his men had hidden well, guided by the civilian Doyle Birchfield. After much argument, the captain had agreed to the guide's plan and brought only nine men with him.

"Any more'n that and we'll make sich a fuss they'll know about you bein' here. Ten men's enough," Birchfield said. "That way we got a good chance o' takin' Tobe Kirkwood and I kin claim the reward."

The captain looked at the gloating mountaineer now and disliked him even more; a ratty-looking individual if he ever saw one, probably no better than the guerillas they were trailing. Out only for the money, no feeling of real loyalty to the country or the Union, just the money. The captain was disgusted by the whole thing; only going along in an attempt to capture this feared Rebel bushwhacker.

Through field glasses, the captain watched the road as the morning wore on. It was crisp and clear and he was glad it was not summer yet. These summers in the South were bad, he thought, with the gnats and mosquitoes and flies of various kinds, all buzzing around one's head.

An ambush like this in June would be unbearable, but in March it was not bad. They waited for several hours.

Hattie June Rose had ridden up the road first, alone, at about eleven o'clock. The captain had looked at his big silver timepiece and confirmed it. They were well back in the woods on a low ridge, far enough away that the horses would not signal each other, the guide had insisted on that.

"Tobe Kirkwood may have some of his men with 'im, maybe he'll be alone like he's supposed to," the guide said. "If he's by hisself, we mite ort ta' shoot him on the road, just bushwhack him and be done with it."

"He's the outlaw, we're not," the captain said drily. "If he comes alone, we'll let him join her inside the house and take him then. When he sees he's surrounded, he may surrender without a shot."

"Oh, ther'll be shots all right," Birchfield said. 'You kin count on that."

"I'm not convinced," the captain replied. "I've seen some of these desperate bushwhackers give up meekly, like a lamb, when they're cornered."

The sound of a horse's hooves on the road drew their attention then and they turned to look. It was Tobe Kirkwood, alone on his red horse. The guide got visibly nervous, his hands shook, at the sight of the mounted man over a half-mile away.

"I've guided you'uns here to him," he now whispered to the captain, his legs turning to water at the thought of facing that awful rider. "If you'uns git 'im, I'm due the reward fer makin' it happen. I think I'll just stay here 'til it's over. I put that rag on the bush like she tole me, ever'thing's set."

The captain sneered at the fear of the guide and shook his head watching the lone guerilla leader ride on toward the house. When Kirkwood was out of sight, he gave his men their final orders.

"The trap is set and we'll spring it in a few minutes. I don't want to wait long, they might flee for some reason. Now that they're in our grasp, there's no reason to tarry.

"This girl, they tell me, has been an accomplice to Kirkwood all along. I want Kirkwood dead or alive and we're going to capture the girl, too. Heck, if she gets shot in the meantime, there's no harm in that."

***

The old house loomed above her as Hattie rode into the weed- grown yard. It had never been painted and had blackened with the passage of years, but in its day had been a handsome country house. It was two-story, with a porch all the way across the front and still in fair shape. The last occupants had died of a strange fever and nobody wanted to live in it, fearing both the fever and the haints that surely stayed in a place like this.

There were bushes in the yard, not neatly trimmed now, but straggly with uncontrolled wild growth. On one of these shrubs a strip of white cloth fluttered limply in the morning breeze. It meant that armed Yankees in blue uniforms were waiting in the woods, waiting to seize and kill Kirkwood. Her heart began to beat wildly at the thought and she brought it under control, calmed herself for the confrontation ahead.

Her thoughts strayed from the violence ahead, even though she welcomed it and tried hard to concentrate on it, but the baby inside her kept coming back to her mind, again and again. What would she do with a baby? she thought. She hated the baby, it was something vile from Tobe Kirkwood, something of his that would come out of her, something growing inside of her.

Forcing herself to face what was coming, she tied her horse at the rear of the house, out of sight, and took her bag of food inside. She had with her also a large handbag, slung over her shoulder, with the hanging rope neatly coiled inside and her father's pistol.

If I ever got the chance, I could shoot him myself, she thought, knowing she did not have the nerve. *He is so strong, so fast, if I miss or even if I hit him and just wound him, he'll kill me on the spot. Better to let the soldiers do it.*

She put the food on the floor in the main living room of the old house, for the time being, and looked around through the other rooms. *Tobe will be furious when he sees the Yankees,* she thought, *and I need to run at that moment.* She opened the door to the upstairs, a door which swung inward from the living room. *Good, she thought, I could run through here and maybe pile furniture or wedge a stick or something to hold this door shut and he couldn't get me then.*

But luck was with her, the door which sealed off the stairs not only opened inward, but had a wooden bar on the stair side of it. Perhaps two families had lived in this house, she thought, maybe a married daughter upstairs and they put this bar on the door for privacy

At any rate, she planned to dash for the door, bar it behind her and flee upstairs at the first sign of the Yankees arriving. Tobe would be crazy with rage and it would be directed at her, it wouldn't take him long to figure it out.

Shortly the red horse appeared in the yard, bearing Big Tobe Kirkwood to his Sunday dinner engagement. He looked at the rag on the bush and grinned, good ole Hattie, always careful in her planning. Her mount would be tied out back, but he might as well tie his in front, it was more convenient. He left the rifle in the scabbard, but entered the house with the sawed-off shotgun in his hands.

There was a little furniture left in the house, thieves had carried off most of it. She had spread the dinner on a rough table and there were two chairs set on opposite sides of the table, the rich greasy smell of fried chicken now filling the room.

He put the shotgun across the seat of one of the chairs and opened his arms for her. She was stiff with apprehension and nerves, but she came to him and they embraced.

"Y'ain't gonna shoot me, are ya', Hattie?"

"No, and I hope you won't shoot me. You've already shot enough of my family."

"I never done it, girl. I swear I never done it. Some o' th'men were a-shootin' and I begged 'em to stop, but they got carried away an' killed ever' one o' them boys."

It was a lie and they both knew it, but she did not reply and he hoped she believed him so he plunged on. "I never knew yore brother was in that bunch. You'd told me somthin' about him, but I'd forgot it." He grabbed her hungrily and pulled her to him, fumbling for her breasts with his hands and holding her to him so she could feel the hardness in his pants. "Hattie, I shore have missed ya'."

"Wait," she said, pushing him away and hoping the soldiers would come soon. "Wait 'til we've eaten, this chicken's getting cold."

She sat down then, leaving him standing alone and awkward in the middle of the floor. He paused for a moment and then took the other chair at the table, laying the shotgun on the floor beside him. She could see the butts of two pistols under his coat.

"Look what I brung ya'," he said, grabbing a chicken leg with one hand and putting the other in his coat pocket. "It's a nice gold watch and you kin keep it with that tintype I give ya'."

He had given her a picture of himself taken in Tennessee before they met and she kept it in the handbag, still slung around her shoulder. He now handed her the watch he had taken off the dead Payne at the Copperhill ferry, a Masonic emblem fastened to the chain. she admired the timepiece.

"Thanks Tobe, it's real nice," she said, dropping the gift into the handbag on top of the hanging rope and pistol. "I'm proud to have that."

"We went raidin' down in Georgie," he said between mouthfuls. "I got it off a feller down there. Boy, this is good chicken."

Before they finished, they heard hooves in the distance. Their eyes met, but she gave no sign of fright or surprise and he seemed calm.

"That may be some o' th' boys. They know where we're at and they may be comin' out to see ya', too."

He picked up the shotgun and walked out on the porch to have a better look. She sat where she was and watched him through the open holes where windows had been, vandals had broken out the glass long ago. Then silently she got to her feet and opened the door into the foot of the stairs, turning quickly and barring it behind her. Now she was safe.

The blue-uniformed troopers galloped into the brushy yard yelling and cursing and Tobe Kirkwood dived for cover, back into the house as heavy lead bullets peppered the porch around him.

"Hattie, goddamn ya', I'll kill ya' fer this," he roared and ran to the closed door to the stairs, finding it barred against him. "I'll cut y'er damn heart out fer this, girl." He pounded on the door with his big fists until it made the whole house rattle, but the bar held.

Instinctively shrinking away from the shuddering door, Hattie backed up the steps and suddenly saw ragged holes appearing on her side of the door. He was shooting through the door, shooting at her with his pistols, trying to put lead into her body.

"Ya' goddamn bitch, lyin' bitch, shittin' whore," he cursed and spittle dotted his red beard. Both pistols were in his hands and he pumped bullet after bullet through the stairway door.

Hattie dashed up the stairs to the second floor and ran to an open window to look out. "Kill him, kill him," she screamed at two bewildered-looking officers in the front yard. "He's right down there, kill him before he gets away."

The two officers, the captain and his lieutenant, were still mounted. They had ordered the rest of the men to go to the back, where Kirkwood would surely flee, and keep up a steady fire into the house. The captain said he wanted them to wound the man while he was pinned in the house and then they would go in after him, or better yet kill him by firing continually into the house.

Their bullets were drilling all through the first floor and Tobe Kirkwood soon had to forget Hattie for the moment and concentrate on surviving and fleeing this deadly trap she had devised. He dove for the floor and rolled up against a wall, thinking hard. Through the windows he could see two officers on horses in the front yard and there seemed to be seven or eight men firing steadily from hidden positions at the rear of the house.

His own red horse had been untied and taken away by one of the arriving Yankees. He had to do something fast or they might rush the house, even charging in on horseback. That damn Hattie had fixed him good, that was plain.

Suddenly an idea hit him and he knew it was his only chance. He unbuttoned his thick winter coat and re-buttoned it around the back of one of the straight chairs they had been sitting in when the attack began. It was not a good dummy, but it looked strangely man-like and would draw temporary attention.

Now picking up the shotgun, he was ready.

Kirkwood scuttled toward the open front door and

threw the coat-wrapped chair onto the front porch, toward his right. It drew the attention of the two mounted officers for a split-second and that was enough.

Their heads turned to follow the strange object clattering across the porch and out of the side of their vision, they saw a tall man instantly appear in the doorway with a shotgun already leveled on them. They tried to turn, but it was too late. Kirkwood pulled the triggers on both barrels at almost the same time, the searing buckshot taking both men in the chest and tearing them from the saddles.

Big Tobe Kirkwood then ran down the steps, dropping his empty shotgun in the flight, mounted the nearest Union horse and frantically rode off.

Hattie saw his escape from her upstairs vantage point and was heartsick. *He'll kill me,* she thought. *He'll kill Granny, he'll kill this awful baby inside me, he's a devil.*

Downstairs the soldiers rushed the house from the rear and found no one, just the remains of a meal. In the front yard they found the carnage of their own officers lying dead and one horse missing. It was all so sudden and final.

"Quit eatin' that chicken and look around this place," said the sergeant, who had now taken command. His men were grinning and picking through the leftovers of the picnic. They had suffered no casualties, not even a scratch.

"This guerilla was supposed to be meetin' with a girl. Her horse is still out back. Anybody see her run? Where'd she go?"

They soon found the barred door, obviously leading upstairs.

"What's the matter?" the sergeant asked, "What's holding it? Is it nailed shut?"

They felt the door give a little and figured, rightly, that it was secured from the inside. They hollered for the girl to come down, but she did not; there was no sound at all from the upstairs.

Finally, the sergeant gave the order for his men to break down the door and they did, hitting it with their rifle butts and shoulders until it caved inward.

It was then they jerked away the splintered door and found Hattie June Rose twisting slowly in the stairwell, having hanged herself with the rope she had brought for Big Tobe Kirkwood.

Chapter Nine

Big Tobe Kirkwood rode into the guerilla camp on the Yankee officer's horse, wild-eyed and near panic. The dark horse was lathered in white foaming sweat, having been run more than four miles over rough country from the old house.

His empty pistols were in the holsters, but his long guns were gone, his coat was gone and his hat was also missing. His long red hair had been blown in all directions by the furious pace of his escape and he had the general appearance of a terrified victim.

"What's the matter, Tobe, where's ya' hoss?"

"Where's ya' coat an' hat, man? Where's Hattie?"

He practically fell off the stolen horse as they gathered around and examined the Union Army markings on the saddle and gear.

"That goddamn Hattie," he snarled, spit flecking his beard in shiny spots. "She had the Yankees there, regl'r uniformed soldiers, 'bout fifty of 'em, and they nearly got me. Damn, they almost had me; hemmed up in that ol' house jus' like she planned it -- the hateful slut."

There were several bags of stolen goods the bushwhackers kept at one side of the camp, under an oilcloth cover to protect them from the weather. Kirkwood went now to this common commissary, to replace his missing hat and coat. He rummaged through the bags of stuff and found a cap and coat, putting them on in a hurry.

"We gotta get outta here," he snapped. "They're probably on the way to raid this camp right now. Hattie's told 'em about it, f'er sure, she'll put 'em on us, boys, we gotta move."

"By the way, Tobe, we got word this mornin' right after you left that there's a reward on you now. The Yankees have put out a $5,000 reward for ya', dead er alive."

"That does it, f'er damn sure. It means ever'body 'roun here will be lookin' to turn me in, f'er the money. I'm gone, headin' f'er the West. Them that want to go with me can go, them that want to stay can stay. There ain't nuthin' worth robbin' left around here anyway."

He dived back into the sacks of stolen stuff and found two good blankets, which he tied on the Union saddle of the stolen horse.

"I mean it," he said. "Get ready to ride. Out West nobody knows us and the reward on me won't mean nothin'. The Yankees almost killed me last year, half m'ear shot away, and they come in a hair o' gettin' me this noon. The War's over with, the Yanks have won and, boys, by God I'm gone."

He was reloading the two cap-and-ball revolvers as he spoke, carefully pouring powder into each chamber and ramming the lead balls home, then topping the cylinders with fresh copper caps. With his now-loaded pistols back in their holsters, he mounted for the ride out; took one of the Spencers from one of the guerillas, to replace the one he lost with the red horse.

Tobe Kirkwood glared at the Fosters and for a moment thought about shooting the both of them just because of their lifelong friendship with the girl. But both of them were good shots, they read his mind and kept their hands close to their own guns while he talked. He decided against it.

"Tell Hattie, by Ned, I'll kill'er fer this," he said, staring at the Fosters. "I'll come back next week er next year, I ain't sayin' when, but I'll come back when she ain't expectin' it, I'll kill that bitch if it's the last thing I do."

***

The Negro girl had walked to town by herself the first time as a free person and it had felt so good, so very good to be in Murphy on her own with nobody to answer to and no set time to be home. She just walked around and looked at things and whistled a tune to herself.

That first day she had no place to stay, so after a while she went back home, home to the Harshaw farm and back to the slave cabin where she lived. The big house, magnificent for the mountains, overlooked a thousand acres of level Hiwassee River bottomland and the slave cabins were clustered around it, like chicks around a mother hen.

But Venus was a slave no longer and she knew it, and she let everybody else know it, too. She said she was leaving, as soon as she found a place to stay in town, and she meant it.

"Oh, Venus honey, tha's jus' foolishness," Miz Harshaw said to her. "Of course y'all are free, all of y'all are free, but we'll pay you to stay and work for us. I need you, honey, stay here and work."

Miz Harshaw reeked of the lilac water she drenched herself in each morning and her kind old wrinkled face was chalky white from the powder she applied liberally to it. Venus loved the old white woman, but she loved even more the freedom. She had to have it and she had no intention of living like a slave, like the slave she had been for all of her sixteen years.

Some of the blacks were staying on the farm, working for wages now and living in the same slave cabins, but two of the families had moved to Murphy and built themselves cabins on the edge of town. She planned to stay with one of these families and maybe even move away from Murphy, go somewhere else, the whole idea of freedom and travel made her light-headed.

"I'll tell you when I'm ready to go, I'm not quite ready yet, but I'm going," she said.

"Oh, honey, I wish you wouldn't," Miz Harshaw said, falling back on her bed. "This house is so big to keep clean and you're such good help, I just pure hate to lose you."

Venus left the bedroom then and began to clean and dust in the master's study. They had told her that she was named for one of the women in one of the books that filled the shelves and lay everywhere in disarray around the room. The master was a kindly man who read and wrote letters and was interested in every plant and every animal on the farm.

He was also very old and very confused by all this freedom business. He paid his ex-slaves very little and had managed to keep most of them and get in a crop of sorts, but it had been hard. These days were hard and he sat and brooded a lot.

"Venus, you don't have to clean right now," he said gently. "Bring us some tea, please, into the dining room."

She went to the kitchen and, along with the cook, brewed a pot of sassafras tea. It was a poor substitute for the good English tea the Harshaws had enjoyed before the War, but this natural drink, made from a tree in the woods, was now just as familiar to them as the real tea had been.

Miz Harshaw was dressed now and she and the master sat at the big table and enjoyed this morning ritual. Venus served them both and then stood and talked with them. They did not invite her to sit down. She would probably not have been comfortable sitting with them.

"So tell us, Venus, when are you leaving us?" the master asked.

"I'm wanting to go Saturday, if it ain't raining."

"You'll have to walk," he mused. "The weather could be a problem for you."

"I'm gonna move in with Charley and his family."

"Yes, Charles is a good man. We hated to lose him."

The Negro known on the farm as Charlie, and now in town as Charlie Harshaw, took more than the master's surname with him. Reared on the farm, he was a natural mechanic and had been trained over a lifetime of blacksmithing and general repair jobs until he was priceless. Charlie could fix anything, from mending leather harness to forging plow points to shoeing horses. He could also make a shoe-mold, or anything else needed out of wood, and then turn around and make a slave (or a white man) a pair of good leather shoes on it. He was good with his hands, quick with his mind, and the farm already missed him sorely.

"You've been a good and faithful servant, Venus, we shall miss you," the master continued. "I'll drive you in Saturday in the buggy. You'll probably have a bundle of things anyway."

And so it went. Miz Harshaw sniffed a little and got teary-eyed some, but she went through a bunch of old stuff in the attic and in old trunks and gave Venus several old dresses that had belonged to a daughter long-gone and married and living in Savannah, they said.

"You might as well take this little trunk, too, to keep your belongings in," she said, giving the light-brown girl a small leather- bound trunk. "Put these two blankets in the bottom."

Come Saturday morning, Venus had a trunk full of stuff, including a butcher-knife liberated from the kitchen. Miz Harshaw bawled out loud now and hugged her and the old woman's tears got on her face and Venus thought she might even cry herself, but she didn't. She looked back one time at the big house and the big river bottom-lands and then anxiously looked out the road toward Murphy.

She had made her own arrangements with Charlie and his wife, but she saw the master give Charlie some money. Charlie was actually her uncle, she knew that, but kinship among the slaves was a casual thing. She was lighter-colored than Charlie or his wife, both of whom were dark and short. Of medium height, Venus could look down on both of them and could certainly look down on their brood of dark children, the oldest about ten.

"Y'll hav' to sleep on the floor, girl, with the rest of the young'uns," Charlie's wife told her and stared suspiciously at the trunk.

"A house-girl ain't too proud to sleep on the floor, are ya'?"

"No, that'll be fine, "Venus said and tried to smile. "I'm just happy to be free, really free."

"Th'ain't nuthin' free in this world, girl," the woman told her harshly. "Charlie has to work harder now than he ever done on the farm in slave times. He's off shoe'in hosses er makin' shoes fer people er somethin' all the time."

Through Charlie, Venus was hired at a white woman's house in Murphy to clean up and cook, but the living arrangement at Charlie's house lasted less than a week. Venus was not really surprised, she had felt the wife's animosity toward her since the beginning.

"Get outta here," the wife told her one morning. "Just get out. I don't like the way Charlie's been lookin' at you, you yaller whore. Get yer stuff and be gone by the time I get back today."

Venus winced, she had never been called yellow or a whore, but she moved out. She found her butcher-knife was missing, but reclaimed it from the cabin kitchen and got all her belongings packed back in the trunk. It was small and carrying it on her shoulder, she managed to take it to the house where she worked and hide it in the woodshed.

She slept in the woodshed for three nights, until the woman of the house discovered her and made her move out, although she kept the job. So Venus moved downtown to an alley and slept in an old carriage house for another night or two until she met Ol' Molly.

"I see ya' in the mornin', comin' outta there," Molly said. "I don't miss much, I know ever'thang goes on in Murphy-town. Where ya' come from?"

"Harshaw Farm," Venus said. She liked this rough white woman, a husky-voiced stocky creature who cussed like a man and sold stuff on market day in the streets. Everybody knew Ol' Molly. "I got a job workin' for a lady up the street."

"You kin stay with me fer a while," Ol' Molly said. "I get lonesome sometime. I got a good place to stay."

And it was a good place, a shed behind one of the stores which had been converted by Molly into a shack, fronting on a downtown alley. Evidence of her profession was everywhere, bits and pieces of Murphy life scattered around on the ground around the shack: broken furniture, mismatched wagon wheels, pots and pans, anything other people no longer wanted had wound up here.

"I fix up a lot of this stuff and sell it," she explained. "I got a cart there I kin push myself, makes it easier t'move stuff. Ya' kin use it if ya' want to, to get y'r trunk down here."

Venus pushed the cart up to the old carriage house and loaded the trunk on it and pulled it behind her back to Ol' Molly's place. It was a lot easier than carrying it, she admitted, this old woman knows how to do things.

Ol' Molly knew where the work was, too, and Venus soon found herself involved in all sorts of tasks. They cleaned houses, swept out stores and lawyers' offices, took care of the sick and old, and constantly traded, always looking for something which could be sold.

Ol' Molly admired her new companion's work habits, a good strong girl who never complained.

"All the niggers are free now and tha's all right with me, I guess," she observed. "Ol' Lincoln, he set the niggers free."

"Don't call me that," Venus said sharply. "I don't like that word and you cain't say it around me now. I'm free, I can go anytime I want to and you cain't call me that no more."

Ol' Molly lifted an eyebrow, said nothing. She also liked the colored girl's spunk.

***

On the head of the Killian Branch, the shooting around the old house had been sharp for several minutes and then it stopped. When it stopped, Doyle Birchfield rode slowly down out of the woods toward the house to see what had happened. His hiding place had been well above and behind the house and he entered the rear yard first, seeing Hattie's horse still tied there.

He rode around the big house to the front yard, where the soldier activity seemed to be. He would tell that smart-talking captain that it was his reward, that Doyle Birchfield and nobody else had led them to their man and now it was over. The Kirkwood reward money was due him. He would probably have to ride all the way down to Cleveland to get his money; would be well worth it.

He realized there were bodies on the ground as he rode into the front yard. From his horse, he looked down and saw that one of them was the arrogant captain with about ten holes leaking dark blood from his chest, staring upward, quite dead.

Birchfield tied his horse and walked up the steps onto the porch.

A Union sergeant walked out of the house to meet him.

"You'uns get Kirkwood?"

"Hell no, killed our officers and rode off."

"What?!"

"Hell yes, we shot the place to pieces and thought we had him, but he's gone and both the officers are dead."

"Where's the girl?"

"In here, come and look."

Birchfield had entered the house where the Union soldiers had cut the hanging rope off Hattie and laid her on the floor in the room where the fried-chicken smell still hung heavily. In fact, one of the soldiers was still gnawing on a chicken bone, the grease shining on his chin.

"Is she dead, too?"

"Nope, she's still breathin' purty good. That rope 'bout done her in, she's got bad marks on her neck and she ain't come to yet, we cain't talk to 'er."

The soldiers had laid Hattie out rather modestly, making an attempt to straighten her skirt and cover her legs with it, but the sergeant pointed and lifted the skirt a little so Birchfield could see her bloody legs and shoes.

"I don't know where all that blood come from," he said. "She may o' got hit by a bullet, either one o' ours or one o' his. Looks like he shot that door all to pieces tryin' to kill 'er before he left."

***

After Kirkwood and his faithful departed, the rest of the guerillas left camp in a hurry. If the Yankees were indeed bent on raiding the camp that very afternoon, they would find it empty.

Some said they would camp further back in the mountains, some were going back to their homes, they all needed some sort of plan.

"Tobe may come back, there ain't no tellin' what he'll do. Soon's he goes down in Georgie er Alabama f'er a week er two, he might come back. "

"Naw, I think he's gone. The War's 'bout over; we'll hang out here fer awhile," the younger Foster said. He seemed to be in charge now. A cool-headed youth who never wavered, he was liked by the men and they listened to him.

"Hattie kin come back now, she can spy for us and

she's a good thinker," he said. "We'll git by all right."

"Go wherever you want to go," he told the rest, "hide out for a few days and we'll meet back here with Hattie by the end of the week". They nodded and left.

"Let's me and you ride out to Hattie's house and see what's happening," he said.

The other riders had left and took anything of value with them, the Yankee soldiers would find nothing if they came.

The Fosters stayed off the roads and went through the woods, fording the Hiwassee River in a secret spot and approaching the Buck Rose farm from the rear. Tying their horses in the woods, they sneaked in and hid in the barn, watching the house. Smoke rose lazily from the rock chimney, Granny was apparently alone in the house. Hattie's horse was gone.

Then they heard and saw the wagon approaching.

It was being driven by an old man they recognized as a Home Guard. The lone horseman escorting the wagon was Doyle Birchfield, a known Union man who was only rarely seen. Hattie's horse was tied to the wagon's tailgate, trotting along behind.

The Fosters dropped down from their vantage point in the barn loft and ran out to see what was in the wagon. Was Hattie dead?

Granny beat them to the wagon and looked over the side, reaching in to touch her grand-daughter gently. They dashed in to join her, keeping an eye on the treacherous Birchfield.

Hattie lay unconscious on a bed of straw in the worn wagon bed, so pale and small in the sunlight, her hair matted with the straw and dried blood caked on the dress tangled over her legs. Her breast rose and fell and she moaned once. She was still alive, but barely.

"What happened to Hattie? Is she shot?"

Birchfield shook his head and dismounted, to stand and face the Foster brothers on the ground. He was nervous and spoke rapidly.

"I think she'll be all right. She tried to hang herself, the soldiers found her and cut 'er down in time. I ain't looked at her, but I don't think she's shot."

Granny and the Fosters picked her up and carried her gently into the house. She was limp, totally helpless in their hands.

"Here, put 'er here on this bed," Granny said. "I'll clean 'er up and look 'er over, see if there's a bullet hole anywheres. You'uns wait outside."

The Home Guard went back to Murphy and the Fosters stood in the yard and talked to Birchfield. It was a cold standoff, two against one, but his kindness toward Hattie had bought his life and all three men knew it.

"She wanted Kirkwood dead for killing her brother," he told them, "and that's how we got together. There's a big reward on Kirkwood now, offered in gold by the Yankees, and everybody will be after him for it. She didn't want the reward, she just wanted him dead and I think she was real afraid of him.

"The soldiers come up from Copperhill and had him hemmed in the house, along with her. She had planned it and Kirkwood must have known it right at the last because he was trying his best to shoot her before he run. Killed two officers slick as a whistle and rode off clean.

"She locked herself upstairs and that's where they found her a-hanging. Reckon it was too much for her to think about, knowing Kirkwood would kill her for what she done to him."

"Tobe shouldn't have killed th' little boy, her brother," the younger Foster said. "He never had no business doin' that, but he done it and nobody could stop him. He goes wild when he starts shootin' an' he just shoots ever'thang in sight, like a hurt rattler a-strikin' at anythang near it."

"Tobe's gone, gone fer good," the other said. "You kin tell the Yanks that, but the rest of us ain't, we're still right here."

"The soldiers are gone to Copperhill with their dead," Birchfield said stoutly. "They'll be back, you kin count on that."

"Tell 'em to come on back and be damn quick about it," the younger Foster said, temper rising. He grabbed the front of Birchfield's shirt with his left hand and reached for his pistol with his right. "I'm a good mind to kill ya' right now."

"Hold it," the other brother said, grabbing the younger Foster's arm and glaring at Birchfield. "The only reason we ain't already shot ya' is ya' brung Hattie back. Next time it'll be different. Now git."

The word travelled slowly but steadily and it was several days, maybe a week, before the botched ambush of Tobe Kirkwood became common knowledge. When it did, hard Union men came to Birchfield and wanted to go finish off Hattie June Rose.

Ragged rough men, as tough as their Confederate opponents, they slipped in after darkness and wanted to hear the story from Doyle Birchfield, who was there when it happened. And they wanted his blessing on their desire to ride up the river and choke the life out of the injured girl.

"That bloody bitch set up the bushwhackers fer the massacre at Evans Mill, I'll bet my hat on it," one of them swore. "Two o' my cousins died out there, never even found th'r bodies."

"We oughta go out there an' settle her hash, once and fer all," another said. "That sassy wench wuz Tobe Kirkwood's eyes all along, the butcherin' red-headed bastard."

Birchfield shook his head and warned against it.

"Kirkwood's gone," he said, "plumb scared out of this country, but the trash he left behind is out there at the house with her, she's the leader now."

"I seen and talked with the Foster brothers," he told his visitors grimly, "an' the rest of 'em are in the barn er the woods. Go if ya' want to, but I want no part of it. Ya'll be shot to rags long 'fore ya' get to the house."

***

On the tenth day after her near-death, Hattie stirred and moaned frequently and Granny took it as a good sign. The old woman was about worn out from the constant care of the girl, who had to be fed broth by hand and her bed-clothing changed like a baby. Hattie had nearly died from loss of blood, she had lost the baby in a convulsive struggle against the rope and the old woman had been unable to make the bleeding stop.

It finally had stopped by itself, after several days, and the old woman then thought the girl would die, she was so weak and pale. Each morning Granny went and hovered over her bed, thinking she would find a young corpse, another of the family to bury, but each morning Hattie's breath came shallow and steady and the girl made it through another day.

The Fosters slept in the barn, but Granny cooked for them and this also put a strain on the old woman, fixing for two grown men. They kept watch night and day and she often did not know exactly where they were, but felt better because she knew their fast-shooting Yankee rifles were somewhere in the woods near the house or up in the barn loft, watching over her like she watched over Hattie.

Birchfield's warning had kept the Unions away for now, but it was only a matter of time until they came. The Fosters knew the danger and kept an eye on the old camp in the mountains. When it was obvious that no Yankee soldiers were coming back for awhile, the guerillas set up camp as before and from the main camp, sent men daily to help the Fosters guard Hattie.

Now Hattie was tossing and whimpering in her bed and Granny fluttered over her like a mother bird, touching her grand-daughter's hands and soothing her brow with a wet rag. Hattie blinked her eyes and woke up, looking straight at her grandmother.

" Where am I?"

"Y're right here at home, child, rest easy."

"Where's Pa? "

"Y'er Pa's gone, honey, so's y'er brother."

Realization showed on the girl's face like a physical presence and she knew all then, the old woman could tell. Hattie bit her lip thoughtfully and looked around the room.

"Granny, I'm so weak I feel like I'm made out of water. Tobe got away, didn't he?"

"Yeah, honey, he went and left, they said."

"Granny, I felt so awful when he got away, I tried to kill myself. He was gettin' away and I knew he'd come back and get me. An' I had that awful baby of his inside me, it was just more than I could bear."

"Hush, hush, it's all right now. You're fine. Ya' lost that baby and near bled to death."

"Am I gonna live, Granny?"

"I think so, child, just rest easy. The Fosters and some o' the other men are here a-guardin' us."

Hattie lay on her back then and stared upward at the rafters. *So Tobe is gone,* she thought, *but gone where. He could come back at anytime to kill me and they would never be able to stop him. Here I lay, weak as a sick kitten, no help to anybody, can't even help myself.*

Granny went outside to fetch the Fosters, let them talk to her, but when they returned, she had slipped into a coma again, breathing better, but unconscious.

"She's gonna make it, Granny," the younger Foster said. "If she talked to you, it's good. She's gettin' stronger, don't ya' think?"

"I don't know," Granny said, shaking her head. "She might just make it, but I'm afraid as weak as she is, she'll come down with a fever o' th' lungs so she cain't breathe good and that'll finally kill her. She's just so weak."

Granny needed assistance, so she told the Fosters to go to Murphy and talk to Ol' Molly. "Send somebody to help us."

Hattie spent another week in a coma and then woke up suddenly one morning and looked upward.

She found herself staring right into another human face, but it was chocolate brown. She naturally thought she was in Hell.

Chapter Ten

Hattie looked around and reality slowly settled on her, she was lying in Granny's big bed in their cabin, but the colored girl was puzzling, a stranger in their house.

"Who're you?"

"My name's Venus."

"What are you doin' here?"

"I'm takin' care o' you. Molly sent me."

Granny came into the room then and hugged Hattie. "So glad to see you awake ag'in, girl. Let's prop you up a minute."

Boosted into a sitting position by the pillows, Hattie talked and listened and did not lapse into a coma again. The next day, with their help, she walked weakly to the outhouse and assisted them later in bathing her frail, pale body.

The colored girl brought chicken broth and cornbread, both in large quantities, and eagerly fed her charge. "Eat this," she commanded and poked it into Hattie's mouth with a big spoon.

"Wuz you really in the War?" she asked Hattie, having heard stories from Ol' Molly and Granny. "A girl in the War, shootin' and ridin'?"

Gathering strength, Hattie rebelled the third day and insisted on feeding herself. "Gimme that," she snapped at Venus, taking control of the spoon. "I can feed myself now."

Bowing to authority, Venus handed it over, but continued to help with the cooking and brought the food to the bed. Hattie was too weak to sit up in a chair, but she was eating well.

And with a hand, she could walk to the outhouse.

Venus quizzed her about the War and Hattie told her of the raids with Kirkwood, the ambushing and the killings. The younger girl listened in amazement at the cold tales coming from the lips of this slender maid.

"I've told you all my stories now," Hattie said one day. "Now tell me about you."

Venus told of being born on a farm down in Georgia somewhere, she was not exactly sure where.

"It was a farm that belonged to some white people who are kin to the Harshaws, cousins maybe. I come from there to work on the Harshaw farm here."

"Where's your folks?"

"Don't know. I 'member a mama and a daddy, but they took me away from there when I was real little and I was raised by a slave woman on the Harshaw Farm. Went to work in the big house f'er Miz Harshaw when I was real young."

"Do you wonder about your family?"

"Slaves ain't got much family, got sold around the country like pigs, went here and there, no tellin' where my folks is now."

"But you're free now, that's good."

"Yeah, I'm free and I kin go where I want. I like that, won't never be a slave again."

"How old are you?"

"Sixteen, soon be seventeen. I cain't read, but Miz Harshaw taught me to count purty good."

"I'm nineteen now," Hattie said, musing. 'Seen a

lot for my age, I guess."

***

The Fosters sat on their horses near the site of the old camp west of Murphy and watched the column of armed men coming toward them. On the road below, riding two abreast, the band of intruders came close headed straight for Murphy.

The spy network had picked up the strands of intelligence and brought them to Ol' Molly, who had sent them on to the Rose farm. Hattie knew about the invasion, but was still too weak to ride, barely able now to sit up in a chair for an hour or two each day.

"Ride and check it out," she told them, sending the Fosters out and keeping the other five bushwhackers on the farm. It was a pitiful guard; all they could do at the time.

The spies said the one-eyed man leading the column was a Yankee deserter named Tim Lyons, an Irishman who had gathered a rag-tag gang of thugs and now bushwhacked on behalf of the Union. Encouraged and equipped by Union forces in Cleveland, he had been sent into the North Carolina mountains to retaliate for the raiding done by Kirkwood.

The two officers slain by Kirkwood in the disastrous capture attempt had friends in Cleveland, other federal officers who had grimly bent the rules of war and sent this killer Lyons into the mountains to bring destruction on those who sided with the Rebel cause.

"I count fifty of 'em," the younger Foster said, spitting tobacco juice on the ground as he spoke. "Th'ain't no way o' stoppin'em. We ain't got enough men."

"Yeah, but we kin save Hattie if we have to."

Lyons had camped along the way and the previous night had talked freely around the fire. Local Yankee sympathizers had visited the camp and sold the Lyons raiders corn for their horses and pork for the men. A young man, whose family backed the North, had reported through a trusted friend to Ol' Molly; the young man's pride and deepest feeling being for the South.

This entire transaction had taken place in less than twenty-four hours, so that the Fosters watching the Union bushwhackers from above knew what had been said around their campfires the night before.

"The Home Guard cain't face Lyons and that bunch," Ol' Molly had told the Fosters. "Lyons is saying his orders are to get Tobe Kirkwood, if he can, and make it hard on all the rest that sided with the South. They think he'll burn the Courthouse, fer sure, and maybe all o' Murphy. An' he may go after Hattie."

Kirkwood was gone, the local Yankees would tell Lyons that, but they would probably also tell him about Hattie, Kirkwood's woman. If Lyons turned his raiders up the river toward the Rose farm, they could only run.

Hattie's heart fluttered within her when they told her what was happening. It was the last few days of April and she could sit in a chair for an hour at the time now, but after that was so weak they had to return her to the bed. She was getting stronger, they could all see that, helped by Venus and Granny, but riding a horse was more than she could manage.

They considered their choices and reached a decision. If the raiders came, they would be coming for Hattie and would probably leave the old woman and the colored girl alone, so there was no reason to move them. The Lyons bunch might even burn the house but still they probably would not harm the other two women. They would be looking for Hattie and any of Kirkwood's men, if they came.

"You've got the biggest, strongest horse," Hattie told the older Foster. "If I have to hit the woods, put me in the saddle in front of you, hold me up and we'll ride double. Your horse can carry two better'n anything else we got."

"Not much of a plan," Granny said, "but the best we kin do. We'll dress Hattie and have her ready to go at any time. Some of y'all watch the river road and ride back to tell us if they come this way."

Tim Lyons stayed in Murphy overnight and stole every loose horse and chicken that his thieving men could get their hands on. Local Yankees such as Doyle Birchfield visited his camp and walked through the now-empty Confederate commissary at the jail with great glee. The Home Guards were gone, having wisely left town.

"A girl?" Lyons said. A black cloth patch covered his bad eye and he glared at his visitors with his good one. "You tell me Kirkwood is gone and you want me to ride out to a farm with fifty men and make war on a sick girl?"

He laughed and cursed them for cowards and told them to kill her themselves if they wanted her dead. He wanted Kirkwood and if the red-headed butcher could not be found, he would ride on to Valleytown and raid some more.

***

The next morning one of the Lyons guerillas poured turpentine on the wooden floors of the Cherokee County courthouse and set it ablaze. The citizens stood in shock as the wooden building burned, and with it all their legal records, a pillar of smoke rising high in the sky as the one-eyed leader rode out of town at the head of his little army.

"Ay, God, Tim," said some of his riders, already drinking heavily even at this early hour, "we giv 'em something to remember us by today." On the slopes of Will Scott Mountain overlooking Murphy, the Fosters sat on their horses that morning and watched through a spyglass as Lyons headed away from them and the courthouse burned, black smoke rolling in heavy clouds into the clear blue sky.

Hattie and Venus and Granny gathered on the porch several miles away, where the other two had propped Hattie up in a straight chair and they also saw the smoke rising, and wondered.

By noon the Fosters and the other riders were back at the farm. They had boldly ridden into Murphy soon after Lyons left and went to confer with Ol' Molly, who knew everything.

"Lyons is gone," they said. "Birchfield went to him and tried to get him to come after you, but he cussed them all fer cowards, said he wouldn't stoop to bring war on a girl. He's gone fer good, burnt the courthouse and rode off to Valleytown to steal up there."

***

The month of May passed easily. Granny rummaged around in her various boxes and gourds and found seed to plant a little garden and a good-sized patch of corn.

Early in the month the word spread into the mountains and they heard that the War was really over, that General Lee had signed a surrender paper with the Yankees up in Virginia and it was all done. By the end of the month they began to see soldiers from both sides return to their homes.

Hattie was getting stronger each day, they could see it. The colored girl, who was strong for her age, walked beside her and held her as Hattie took trembling steps around the yard. And after a few days, the trembling stopped and she could walk alone.

The first week in June, she called for her horse and, with help, mounted the side-saddle and rode around the yard some. From then on, she rode each day, bracing herself against the swaying, lurching gait of the walking horse and getting stronger all the time.

She even hoed a little in Granny's garden and began to boss Venus, their former nurse-patient relationship fading away. Hattie June Rose was now firmly in command.

"Bring me that bag," she snapped. "Get that box over there and set it down right here." Venus meekly obeyed.

Hattie went through all her clothes and all her other possessions, taking some sort of inventory. A plan was not formed in her mind completely yet, but it was taking shape and she definitely had travelling in her thoughts.

In the handbag that she had taken to the old house, she found her father's pistol. The hanging rope had also been in that bag, but nobody mentioned it to her; lost to memory, like something that had happened to someone else, a hazy story dimly told and now forgotten.

"Get me some fresh powder and caps," she ordered the Fosters and they did. "I want to see if I can still shoot this thing."

Venus trailed along behind her as they went outside and Hattie expertly loaded the cap-and-ball revolver.

"Set a wood-chip up on that fence post yonder."

Venus ran to do it and then hid behind her young mistress as Hattie leveled the gun, taking careful aim. The pistol barked smoke and flame and the wood-chip flew into the air, falling in the garden.

"Run and get it, Venus, bring it here."

The colored girl darted into the garden and retrieved the wood-chip, which now had a blackened .36-caliber hole in its center. Hattie looked at it and grinned.

"Set two more up, 'she said.

Venus put her fingers in her ears to blot out the sharp report of the pistol and then ran to get the chips, all hit, time after time. When the cylinder was empty, Hattie reloaded it and turned to her companion.

"Want to try it, Venus?"

At first reluctant, Venus gingerly accepted the gun and fired it several times under Hattie's instructions. "There's a little notch in the top of the hammer, see it?" she asked. "When the hammer is cocked back like this, you put the front bead-sight in that little notch and then's the time. Hold the gun on whatever you want to shoot out there, and if the bead's lying in that notch, the bullet will hit whatever the bead's covering. If you hold that bead on that wood-chip, the bullet'll hit the chip."

It was simple, but Venus disliked the recoil and smoke and she flinched when the gun fired. Soon she could hit the chips about half the time and was becoming used to the kick. The pistol was merely a handtool, she could see that. It could not cut like a knife nor sweep like a broom, but it could send a bullet slamming into a target a good distance away. And with it, you could intimidate or hurt another person if that was needed.

"Is this the gun ya' killed the Bradfords with, that ya' told me about?"

"That's it," Hattie said. "The very gun. Held it against their hearts and blew 'em both to Hell." It seemed so long ago, so far away.

"I couldn't never shoot nobody," Venus said.

"Yeah, you could," Hattie said quietly and stared right into the colored girl's brown eyes. It was a look Venus could never forget. "You sure could, 'specially if I asked you to."

A day later she took out the patch of Little Buck's death-shirt stiff with his dried blood, and sat in the rocking chair holding it for a long time. Venus did not understand, but Granny did.

When she put it away, she got out the tintype photograph and the watch with the Masonic emblem on the chain. Venus looked over her shoulder at the picture of Kirkwood, curious.

"That the man y'all talk about?"

"Yeah, that's him all right."

"S'posed to have red hair?"

"Yeah, lots of it."

"Mean, too, they say."

"Mean as a snake, don't ever forget it," Hattie said, staring at the photograph. "We'll be lucky if he don't come back one night and burn the house down on top of us, kill everybody in it. He's pure old Satan, that's for sure."

In mid-July, Hattie was fit as a fiddle and ready to go. She rode into Murphy on Saturday, dressed in black with a feather in her hat, sitting side-saddle and escorted by seven Confederate guerillas armed to the teeth.

"Looks like Hattie June Rose, queen o' th' Kirkwood Bushwhackers survived the big war," one of the onlookers said softly. "Who's that nigger girl sittin' on th' hoss behind her?"

"Don't know, don't ask. Just leave 'em alone."

"Are ya' skeered a' them Fosters?"

"Naw, man," the other quipped. "I'm skeered o' them Spencers."

"Ha, ha, very funny."

They looked over the burned courthouse and promenaded through the market crowd, turning heads in every direction, keeping the horses to a slow, stately walk.

Hattie stopped the mounted procession in front of the wagon where Ol' Molly was selling.

"Get me one of them peaches," she said, turning her head to speak softly to Venus. Every eye in the crowd was on her and they were hushed, some hearing what she said. Venus dropped off the back of the horse and ran toward Molly, who was coming out to greet them with a fresh peach in her hand.

"Good rnornin', Miss Hattie, y're lookin' mighty good today."

"Thank you, Molly, let me pay you for the peach."

"Naw, honey, glad to give it to ya'. You and the men out fer a mornin' ride, are ya'?"

"Need to get some horses shod, Molly, and wanted to check on things here in town."

Venus climbed back on the horse behind Hattie and they rode on. Conversations began in the marketplace again and Ol' Molly was looked at with new respect by the Yankee copperheads, who had hung on every word in the exchange between them.

Daintily eating the peach, Hattie led the parade at a walk down through town to the ex-slave Charlie Harshaw's place. The Negroes visited and chatted while he shoed several of the horses.

"We got any money to pay with?" the Fosters asked.

"Yeah, we got a little," Hattie laughed. "We're not rich, but I hid some and saved it from that time Tobe sold all them horses. I'll pay Charlie."

Back through town they went when the horses were shoed, looking straight ahead and again drawing stares. Two little boys by the side of the road, knowing they were looking at some sort of authority, saluted them.

Hattie smiled and stopped, leaning from her horse to give each of them a coin from her purse. It was a tale years later they would tell their own children, properly embellished.

"I wish we still had Greybeard to track for us," she said when they returned to the farm. "I'd let him find Kirkwood for me."

"Hell, he went with Kirkwood. Him and Tobe wuz big buddies anyway, he'd never of helped you get Tobe."

"I know, I know, I'm just thinkin' out loud. All the Cherokees left with Tobe, didn't they?"

"Yeah, he said he wuz goin' out West and they said most o' th' Indians are in the Indian Territory out there so they'd just go, too."

"We're gonna need some more horses," Hattie said. "Need a horse for Venus and a pistol, too, if y'all can find one to spare. Bring me about four or five good horses."

"Where you want us to go to get 'em?"

"We're heading West, so don't go west to get them. I don't want to ride through country where y'all have just finished stealing their best horses. Go east, over toward Franklin, we never bothered anybody over there."

"How many men? "

"Take everybody you've got. We'll be all right here for a few days. After that little show we gave 'em over in Murphy, they'll be afraid to come for me for a while."

***

In a week they were back with five good horses and two Yankee pistols. "We found a man that had just gotten back from fightin' in th' Yankee army," the Fosters said proudly. "Took these here pistols and one o' th' hosses off him."

Hattie spent another week getting ready to leave, including a secret trip to talk with Ol' Molly. She pressed money into Molly's hand and made her promise to give Granny a decent burial when the time came.

"I'm leaving, Molly, may never come this way again. I got things to do out West."

"Y'll never find him, girl, an' if ya' do, he'll kill ya' first."

"We'll just see about that, maybe he will, maybe he won't."

Molly cried and hugged her. Granny understood and stayed dry-eyed through the whole process.

"Use y'r head, girl, and you'll get him. It's got to be done. Like I tole ya' a long time ago, a woman's not strong like a man, but she kin think and she kin scheme about things. An' she kin use what she's got to persuade a man, nag him, stay after him till he does what she wants done."

"I don't know what man you're talking about, Granny, the one I'm looking for won't listen to me now."

"Y'll find another'un, honey, maybe it'll be one o'

these Fosters, they're good men." Hattie shook her head, the Fosters were more like brothers to her, they had all been schoolchildren once, no romance there.

They found a saddle for Venus and soon had her riding the horse she had picked out, even found a man's old slouch hat for her to wear. The Fosters taught her to load and shoot one of the stolen Yankee pistols and she enjoyed it, laughing with glee when she hit the mark.

Hattie had a talk with the colored girl, which she thought needed to be done.

"Venus, you got a right to know what's going on," she said. "I'm fixing to leave, to go West, and I was hoping you'd go with me, but you don't have to, nobody's forcin' you..."

"I wanna go," Venus said. "I listen, I know what y'r doin' ."

"Well, listen a little bit more. I'm going into places where it's rough and dangerous and I don't care. You can stay here with Granny and Molly if you want to. How do you feel about it?"

"I'm free. Tha's all I keer about. I kin go where I want and don't nobody own me, not even you. I took keer o' you while you wuz sick and I like you a lot. I'm going."

"Good, that's what I wanted to know."

"Don't never call me 'nigger' and don't try to sell me and ever'thang'll be all right. I'm a free girl."

***

The guerillas were not as definite in their choice.

"There's no reason for me to stay here," Hattie told them. "Half this county hates my guts and somebody will finally get me, sooner or later."

"Y're goin' after Tobe, ain't ya'?"

"Yep, that's the size of it."

"We ain't got no quarrel with Tobe."

"Well, I have and I intend to settle it my way."

In the end, the Fosters agreed to go with Hattie and Venus at least part-way. They said they'd probably go to California, always wanted to see the place, and maybe dig for gold. The rest would scatter back to their homes or drift elsewhere, one man indicating that he might stay on with Granny for a while.

Goodbyes were said and the four rode out, leading four extra horses.

Hattie looked back at Granny standing on the porch of the cabin one time and then turned her head toward the West. It was the last time she would ever see the little farm on the river.

"You may never find 'im, Hattie," the younger Foster said. "The West is a big place."

"Yeah, I know, but I know a good place to start the hunt."

***

Three days later, the doctor's wife tended her flowers alone at the big country house near the Ocoee River. Here in Tennessee, the War was officially over and it was the first week of August, 1865.

She would like to visit her relatives in upper Tennessee and see the changes, what damages the War had done to that region, where she had been reared, but her husband, the good doctor, was away nearly all day every day. He came in at night tired and collapsed into bed. The next day would be a repeat, unless the sick were brought to their house and the treatment room he kept there.

If I could only get away for a week or two, it's

been like this for years, she thought. *I'd like to see Chattanooga, see Knoxville.*

There had been bushwhacking by both sides in the country around her, but due to his profession, the doctor's house had been spared. Both sides brought him their wounded and through them, he had learned of the gore and had told her. Yet, no raiders had ever come to the house.

Except, of course, her nephew Tobe. He had come several times and they said he did terrible things, but it was all the War, wasn't it? And besides, most of the devilment Tobe did was over in North Carolina or some other such distant place. So it mattered very little to her.

Now she read her books and letters and pined for better things, the excitement of a city, and tended her flowers, which were doing not too good due to the summer heat.

She worked her way through the two flower beds in the front yard under the crepe myrtle bushes, and then into the narrow flower bed beside the house. This little side yard deserved its own flowers so she had fixed a bed here, between the house and the buggy path.

It was here, kneeling and digging in the loose black dirt, that she stopped to wipe the sweat from her face and a movement to her right at the front of the barn, caught her eye.

The doctor's wife looked in amazement and realized that the two young bearded men were coming toward her, coming out of the barn, in a fast walk that was almost a trot. Neither seemed hurt or sick and she could see rifles in their hands.

"Wait a minute," she said helplessly. 'The doctor's not here…"

She saw that her words had no effect on them, they did not even answer, but kept coming at that relentless pace, getting nearer. She dropped her trowel, dashed around the corner of the house and into the back door where she found herself facing a Negro girl, standing barefoot in the middle of her clean kitchen floor, with a cocked revolver aimed right at her nose.

Chapter Eleven

Hattie had watched the drama unfolding from the woods and by the time she entered the back door, the Fosters had tied the doctor's wife securely in a straight-backed kitchen chair.

She'll show her feelings right away, Hattie told herself. *If she knows I put the Yankees on Tobe Kirkwood, it will show at the first.* She held her head high and walked proudly as she entered the kitchen to greet her captive.

"I know you," the doctor's wife hissed.

"Good morning," Hattie smiled sweetly. "We're glad to see you."

"I bet you are. You've probably come to steal everything I've got."

"No, not exactly. Although that's a good idea and we may have time to do it before we leave."

"I don't recall your name," the doctor's wife said now, resigned to her fate, "but you were with Tobe that time he came here."

"That's right, I was here once. And if you don't recall my name there's certainly no sense in me giving it to you now."

"Tobe would kill you if he was here; he told us about you setting a trap with Yankee soldiers, trying to get him."

"Where is he now?" Hattie broke in, eager for the

answer.

"Don't you wish you knew?"

"Well, if he told you about the Yankees, I know at least he came through here when he left."

"Sure he did, stayed a day with us, but tha's all I'm telling. He's gone now and you'll never know where."

Hattie smiled and looked around the room. This was going to be fun. The woman was arrogant and proud and Hattie would bring her down a notch or two. It was plain that she had more information she was not giving up yet. Hattie had hoped since the start that she could pick up Tobe's trail here through his relatives and now it seemed possible.

She motioned with her head to the Fosters and they stepped out on the back porch with her, leaving Venus to guard the doctor's wife. Hattie quickly gave orders to re-tie the woman, in a more vulnerable position.

Deliberately she waited for several minutes until it was done and then dramatically entered the kitchen again.

"What are you doing with me?" the doctor's wife asked now, tryin to be firm, her voice quavering with fear. "You better let me go, the doctor will be home soon and he will shoot you, all of you."

Venus sniggered at this and the Fosters laughed out loud. Hattie shook her head and said nothing.

"I said let me go, turn me loose this instant," the woman said and then burst into tears at the hopelessness of it all. Being laughed at and tied up in her own kitchen by an uppity nigger girl and three white outlaws. It was a shame she could not bear, yet she was unable to stop it.

Her legs were still tied to the chair, but the young men had tied her arms across the top of the table. She sat now at the table as if she would eat there, her chair tucked neatly under the edge. They had stretched her arms across the surface of the table, tied tightly, so she now faced Hattie with palms upward and arms pulled forward by the ropes, in a position of supplication, almost begging for mercy.

Hattie dragged a chair into place opposite her victim and sat down facing her. The girl even reached across the table and patted her insolently on her bare inner wrists which were turned upward, the pale white skin pinched cruelly by the ropes.

"Don't worry," Hattie said, looking coldly into her eyes. "You won't be hurt if you tell us what we want to know."

"I won't tell you a thing," she sniffed, still sobbing.

"We'll see about that," Hattie said, motioning to one of the men. "Give me your knife."

Slowly the older of the Foster brothers withdrew a big bowie knife from its homemade leather sheath. Hattie grasped the wooden handle of the knife and looked down at the blade, discolored from animal blood and constant rubbing of the sheath. She tested the edge and found it razor-sharp.

"I saw him butcher a hog with this very knife a week or two ago," she said quietly. "And he's stuck it to the hilt in quite a few Yankee guts. I'm giving you one chance and then this blade is ready for you. Tell me where Tobe Kirkwood is."

The doctor's wife looked at the evil knife in Hattie's hand and down at her own pale white arms, stretched by the ropes and ready for butchering. She shuddered as she thought of the blade which had killed men and animals now severing her own flesh. She whimpered, but there was just no escape. She hated this girl, how she hated her.

"I mean to know where Tobe's at," Hattie said to her again, snapping her thoughts in pieces. "Look at me woman, I'm serious."

Horrified, the doctor's wife stared as Hattie calmly grasped the arm in her hand and pricked the inside of her forearm with the sharp point of the big knife. Hypnotized by the spectacle, the woman watched as her own warm blood swelled up out of the puncture wound and ran down the side of her arm, puddling on the table.

"You cut me."

"I sure did and it's fixin' to get worse. I'm planning to cut your fingers off, one at a time. Then I'm gonna split your arms wide open, cut clean to the bone, from shoulder to wrist. Where's Tobe?"

Hattie laid the blade of the heavy bowie across the woman's fingers then and the doctor's wife fainted dead away, her eyes rolling back in her head, sagging against the chair.

"Get a bucket of water," Hattie ordered Venus, who ran to the well and returned with a dripping wooden bucket. "Now, throw it on her head."

The colored girl did as she was told and the water drenched their victim, bringing her back instantly. Water streaming from her bedraggled hair and soaking her dress, the doctor's wife looked like a drowning rat.

"Wake up, sweetie," Hattie snarled in her face. "I want you to be able to see the cuttin' I'm doing."

"I'll tell. Stop. Stop. I'll tell." the woman muttered low. She was broken now, scared out of her wits by this determined girl with the bloody knife in her hand. "I'll tell you."

"So talk, hurry up."

"Tobe's my sister's boy," the woman said quietly, glaring at the girl with anger, knowing the knife could still bite if she did not deliver. "He stayed with us just one night and then went on to Texas. My sister wrote and told me where he's at, but I knew where he was going anyway."

"And where's that?"

"A town called Waco, Texas. We've got a cousin out there, been out there since before the War. He's got a farm and Tobe's working for him."

"So he didn't just wander around the West?"

"No, he didn't wander, didn't have to. He went right straight to his cousin's farm. He might be gone from there now, but that's where he's been this summer."

"You say your sister wrote you," Hattie said. "I want to see the letter."

"Let me loose and I'll go get it," the doctor's wife said, looking down at the ropes and her still-bleeding arm.

"No," Hattie said firmly. "You tell me and I'll find it."

"Look in the top drawer of my dresser, in my bedroom."

Hattie and Venus went rambling through the house then and found the bedroom, soon finding the letter, which Hattie read. It verified the woman's story.

"We'll be leaving you now, ma'am," Hattie said politely. "Your husband can untie you when he gets home. I don't believe you'll bleed to death til then."

"I hope Tobe sees you first, girl," the woman said through clenched teeth. "I hope he kills you, hope he kills every one of y'all for what you did to me."

***

August was warm, good weather for camping out and they spent the nights along the road, cooking over an open fire. They rode through Chattanooga and then into northern Alabama. Everywhere there were signs of the recent War.

Rebuilding the South would take a long time, they could see that. Huge fields had grown up in tall weeds, high as a man's head, left untended for four long years. They saw houses in ruins, farms almost completely reclaimed by the forest, groves of young trees growing in the yards of abandoned homes.

They met roving bands of free blacks, sleeping in the woods like themselves, wandering simply because they were free and had no master to tell them what to do now. Venus stared at these and they stared at her, some begged her for food, she shook her head and rode past them.

The land flattened out quickly when they came down from the high mountains and the days grew hotter than they were used to. Hattie wiped the sweat from her face with a handkerchief and the Fosters both grumbled. "We ain't likin' this heat," they told her, "we belong on higher ground."

"Break away anytime you want," she said. "You don't have to stay with us. We're big girls now, we can look after ourselves."

They stopped in the towns they came through and Hattie bought food for them and rations for the horses from the last of the money from home, the last of Kirkwood's money she had taken when he sold the stolen horses to the Yankees.

"Don't worry," she told them. "We've still got these four horses we're leading, we can sell them when we need to."

Each had an extra mount and they rode them on alternating days so the horses would last longer. It was a system that worked well and they covered lots of ground.

In a nameless town in Mississippi, a high-toned white woman tried to buy Venus from them, with no results.

"Missy, sell me y'h g'ul," she said. Her drawl was slower and heavier than the mountain twang, but they understood her plainly. "M'h slaves all run off. Ah need one t' w'k in th' house."

"She cain't sell me, she don't own me," Venus said loudly. "Nobody does, I'm free and I ain't workin' fer you."

"That's right, lady," Hattie said, amused at Venus. "She's right touchy about that, too. If I were you, I'd walk on and not mention it again."

"Folks cain't buy other folks anymore, slavery's over with," Venus said loudly, staring at the Fosters and daring them to sell her. "Y'all cain't sell me."

"Hush, hush," Hattie soothed her. "Calm down, nobody's gonna bother you."

The Fosters wondered out loud what the future might bring and talked several times with Hattie about where they were going. They had no quarrel with Tobe, although they understood fully her mission. They wanted to see the West and go to California, and preferred to get into the Rocky Mountains as soon as possible. They had no desire to go by way of Texas or see any more heat or flat land than was necessary.

"We don't want to see you hurt or killed either," the younger Foster said.

"I hope to avoid both those possibilities, but I am

determined to find and shoot Tobe Kirkwood, if I can. Beyond that, I've not thought of what might happen or where I might go.

"I realize it's my fight," she told them. "And I don't expect you to take a part in it. I'm the one that's responsible for this and I'll see it through, one way or another. It's that simple. You've been good friends, steady as a rock, and I'll always think good of you both. Leave us anytime you want to. You don't owe us a thing. We been glad to have you this far."

"Y'all ride too fast and too hard," Venus complained. "My butt's sore from all this riding. Can't we stop and stay in one place and rest for a day or two?"

***

In Waco, the marshal ate a good breakfast as usual and strolled around town smoking a fine cigar, as was his habit, seeing and being seen. Townspeople smiled and nodded and spoke to him, he tipped his hat to the ladies and shook hands with the men.

August Stegner was a good politician, in addition to being City Marshal, and he felt it was good business for the people to see him regularly and he believed strongly in law and in order. A former Texas Ranger, he now had a good life as a town lawman and he did not regret that his wild Ranger life was behind him. He liked eating well and sleeping in a clean bed, under a roof, every night.

"Good mornin', Marshal."

"Good mornin', Mayor, looks like another hot one."

"Yeah, maybe rain by the end o' the week, cool things off some."

"The new night deputy's workin' out fine, Mayor,

gonna make us a good man."

"Fine, glad to hear it."

Assisted by five men, Marshal Stegner kept Waco under firm rule. It was the way the mayor and the city council like it. No surprises, no crisis, no problem.

"Heard them gals down in the cribs rolled another drunk last Saturday night," the mayor said, grinning at Stegner.

"Might have. If they did, it ain't nothin' new. Law can't stop everything, can it?"

"Naw, I'm just funnin' ya'. If the only trouble we have in Waco is a whore rollin' a drunk in the cribs, we'll be in purty good shape."

"Thank you, Mister Mayor. Have a cigar?"

"No, Marshal, but thank you just the same. They're bad for my asthma."

Marshal August Stegner proceeded down the sidewalk and paused to look at himself in a store window, using the dusty glass as a mirror. Adjusting his hat and black string-tie, he was pleased.

Look like a town man for sure, he thought, *no doubt about it. The suit, the vest, the hat, this fellow's not riding nor sleeping outside anymore.*

In fact, he had even considered selling his horse. If he needed to travel, he could rent a horse or a buggy at the livery stable, but he continued to keep the horse, maybe as a reminder of the rough Ranger times, paying a monthly fee at the livery stable for his mount's keep.

He'd sell it one of these days, he knew that. His duties were inside the city limits of Waco and a horse was just a needless expense. Marshal Stegner was a businessman and he hated useless expenses.

On his daily rounds he kept close watch on his

own businesses, which paid him far more than the marshal's position did. For Marshal Stegner owned and operated the biggest and best sporting house in Waco and was a half-owner in the finest saloon, where he was headed now. Walking made him thirsty and a beer, on the house, halfway through the morning was his only indulgence in alcohol.

"Mornin', Marshal," the bartender said. "Put it on the table for you?"

Marshal Stegner nodded and sat down at the table in the back corner, his usual place. The bartender brought the mug of beer and set it on the table in front of him. From here, the officer could watch the front door and nobody could get behind him.

His partner Moody was asleep upstairs in his room since he usually worked the night business. He and Moody saw each other about once a week to go over the books. Moody enjoyed the protection of the marshal, a status he had not had in other towns, and therefore kept a straight accounting of the money they made in the saloon. He feared the marshal, as did most folks who knew of him even slightly.

For Marshal Stegner had reached a certain attitude, a certain mental state, in his Ranger days, that made him cool to danger or excitement of any kind. He smiled as needed in meeting people, but he hardly ever laughed. And he never, never got excited. Not over money, not over pretty women, certainly not over danger.

He was calm, no matter what. The other Rangers had known it early and looked to him for assurance and leadership when the bullets flew. Their own adrenaline pumping wildly, their eyes flashing, their faces flushed with blood, the Rangers would rally around Stegner when battling outlaws or Mexicans.

"Set y'r line," he commanded in a fierce battle with Mexican bandits. "Keep a steady fire on those three up in the rocks, they're hurtin' us the most." Raw recruits had done his bidding that day, pinning the best outlaw riflemen momentarily while Ranger Stegner, pistols blazing from both hands, had led a charge that was still talked about today.

Now almost thirty years old and in his prime, Marshal Stegner sipped his daily beer and watched the front door. He had served as a city officer here through most of the War and had never been in the military. Now soldiers were returning from both sides and the giant job had begun of rounding up and organizing the wild herds of Texas cattle which had ranged and bred freely during the past four years of the War.

"Good mornin', Marshal," the two soiled doves said, giggling as they walked past his table and went to the bar for beer. He nodded and spoke, they were employees who served him well. Some of the prostitutes were rotated between working at the big house and here at the saloon, where there were three rooms upstairs which could be used for entertaining customers.

Marshal Stegner used his power to keep any other bordello from doing business in Waco. The big dwelling house had been bought for the very purpose. It stood on a street near the saloon district and the neighbors did not complain. Marshal Stegner did not allow his whores to be loud or to drink with customers and the house was operated in a quiet and tasteful manner. The mayor and other business people were frequent clients at the Stegner house and well-heeled cattlemen also went there regularly.

The rowdier crowd got their sexual tensions relieved in the grubby cribs at the end of the street, where the marshal allowed the independent whores to operate.

"We're bout ready to go back to the big house, Marshal," one of the girls at the bar said. They were sipping beer from mugs, talking to the barkeep.

"We been here over a week and there ain't much goin' on here. We get lonesome f'er the other girls."

"I'll talk to Jo, let you know something tonight."

"Thanks."

Jo was his manager at the big house, an older woman he had met through Moody. She bossed the girls, kept the money and generally ran the house, buying food and clothing for the whores and keeping track of the customers' desires.

Keeping track of Marshal Stegner's desires was much easier. Running whores for him was similar to running cattle, in fact he looked at some of his larger-breasted women sometimes as almost being a type of cattle. They had to be fed and housed and they made him money. It was as simple as that.

Sex for the marshal was a business and he indulged himself only about once a week. Jo usually kept at least one young girl in the house who was just beginning in the business and would arrange for her to be available when the marshal got horny.

"Gonna shoot today, Marshal?" the man on the sidewalk asked.

"Yeah, I better. Might get rusty if I don't," he answered, now on his usual walk to the post office, another part of daily routine.

He fired his pistols regularly, too, with the City of Waco providing powder and lead. Shooting at tin cans in a weedy vacant lot near the center of town kept him sharp.

He knew it and they knew it, the townspeople who depended on him to keep the peace. The sound of his revolvers firing about once a week was part of Waco life.

He wore a pair of matched Navy Colts, one in an open-topped fancy leather holster on his right hip, the other hidden under his left armpit in a slick, silk-lined shoulder rig. They had a natural pointing ability built in, it seemed, and they were light and very fast.

"Why don't you carry a .44?" Moody had asked. "It shoots a bigger bullet, tears a bigger hole in a man. Lots o' these drovers carry a .44." Moody drank too much, it seemed to the marshal, and ran his mouth too much.

"The .44 is too heavy, too slow," he replied patiently. " Here in town all your shooting is going to be indoors or at real close range. These .36-caliber guns are plenty enough to kill a man and they're lighter, which means they're quicker to get out and easier to carry."

Most of the drovers were fair shots with a rifle, lousy shots with a handgun. The former Ranger knew this and based his strategy on it. With his regular practice sessions, he had the edge. He also knew the town well and they did not. Taking advantage of the terrain was another lesson learned well in his Ranger days.

When he was called to a certain saloon or alley or livery stable to settle a quarrel or arrest a bad man, he went in the back way. He had no qualms about drawing his pistols well before he entered, had no intention of being drawn into gunslinging games. He intended to survive.

"Here's your mail, Marshal, not much of it today," the clerk said handing over three letters.

Marshal Stegner walked on to his office, also provided by the City of Waco, attached to a small jail. The regular day deputy was sweeping out the place when the marshal walked in and sat down at his battered desk.

"Mornin', Marshal, what come in the mail?"

"Usual stuff, I reckon, wanted posters from other places. People they want us to look out for. Le's see."

He slit the first letter open with his pocketknife and began to read. It came from Tennessee.

***

It was hot in Vicksburg and they sold two of their horses there, Hattie keeping half the money and the Fosters taking the other half.

"We shore hate to leave you'uns, Hattie."

"We'll be all right, don't worry."

"Well, if it's meant to be, maybe we'll see ya' sometime."

They both hugged Hattie June Rose goodbye and she nearly cried to see them ride away, but they were all grown now and they all had got through a terrible time together. They gravely shook hands with Venus, who was enjoying the third consecutive day of not riding.

"Where they goin'?"

"From here to Arkansas and then on to California. At least that's what they said. They know somebody in Arkansas, but they just want to see what's in California. Maybe we'll go out there, too, sometime."

They crossed the Mississippi on a creaking ferryboat and headed across northern Louisiana, still leading the two spare horses. The first week in September, 1865, they actually stood on Texas soil for the first time and sold the two extra horses to a man who had gold money.

"We'll be fine now," Hattie said. "We got a little money and we can have these horses shod again in the next town we hit."

"Wonder if anybody is lookin' for us out here?"

"No, I don't think so," Hattie laughed. "We're so far from Murphy nobody knows who we are."

"But y'all hurt that old woman and stole some of her stuff," Venus said. "The law might be lookin' for us."

Hattie threw her head back and laughed loudly at the colored girl's fears. "Don't worry," she said. "We're just strangers passin' through, nobody knows anything here, they're just glad the War's over with."

Into the flat country of East Texas they rode, the sage and live oaks looking strange to mountain girls accustomed to seeing mighty chestnuts in vast stands of virgin timber, miles of steep mountains and high rock bluffs. Here was a wide-open country different from anything they'd ever seen.

There were deer and wild cattle everywhere, running through the brush. From time to time, they met bearded riders in pursuit of the longhorned cattle, hazing them into small groups through the countryside.

Hattie got excited and Venus could sense the change in her as they neared Waco. They camped for the last night, sleeping under the stars, knowing they would see the town on the next day.

"What if we see that Kirkwood man first?"

"Aw, we probably won't be that lucky," Hattie said. "I hope to see him first, but it may take a long time to find him, and he may have moved on."

Hattie had little to go on, she knew that, but the recent letter showed that just a few months ago he was at Waco, working with a relative. If she could not find Tobe, she could find the relative and make him tell, if he knew, where Tobe had gone.

Venus was wearing a dress they had taken from the doctor's wife in Tennessee and Hattie had two more in her belongings. They had also taken two frying pans from the woman's kitchen to use along the way. That had been the extent of their looting and she felt no fear from the law, as Venus did, for such a minor incident so far away.

Regardless, she could still feel fear for Tobe Kirkwood, fear and hate, and as she thought of him being near, she instinctively flexed her fingers and looked around.

"Let's shoot our guns, Venus," she said, dismounting. "No harm in a little practice. We might get action sooner than we think."

In a grove of trees, they fired and reloaded their pistols, laughter replacing some of the tension as they got into an impromptu shooting match. The mark was a knot on a dead tree and both made the bark fly around it, though Hattie was quicker and more accurate.

An hour later they rode into Waco and looked around, pacing the horses at a slow walk as they dodged wagons and people on foot, looking at the houses and saloons and buildings. Few people seemed to notice them at all, the white girl riding side-saddle, dressed well and her Negro girl-companion. Both wore pistols in their belts, but even this did not seem out of place, considering the times.

Then in the middle of the street, they were confronted by a tall man in a black suit who grabbed the bridle of Hattie's horse and stopped them.

"Ladies, welcome to Waco, " he said. "You've had a long ride, I'd guess, all the way from Tennessee. I'm Marshal August Stegner and I want you both to step into my office for a little talk."

Chapter Twelve

"Get outta th' goddamn way, Petey."

Big Tobe Kirkwood swore at his dog constantly, the stupid thing insisted on running right beside the wagon horses and often was nearly trampled by them.

I hate going to Waco, he thought to himself. *A fine horse-ridin man like me having to drive a damn team and load a wagon like a damn teamster. This is a fine note for a Rebel guerilla to end up doing, working like a farmhand.*

His cousin was blood-kin, for sure, but he had sided with the Union and gave Tobe a job only because he, too, was originally from East Tennessee and he was still family. The farm was small, only the two of them to do the work and the cousin's wife cooking for them. It was a hell of a disgrace for a free-booting man like Tobe.

The whites had fallen away from him soon after they fled Murphy. The Cherokees, led by Greybeard, had left him for the Indian Nations. So he rode into Waco alone and found his cousin quickly.

The cousin looked hard at the pistols and the lever-action Spencer carbine, and Tobe soon learned the politics of the job. He told no bushwhacker stories and he bit his lip when the cousin spoke favorably of the Union. He would work and rest here for a while and then move on, maybe south to Mexico.

"We need some salt, some flour and other stuff.

Take the wagon and get it, I'll stay here and work on the corral fence," the cousin said. "The woman'll tell you what to get, she's got the money."

The cousin's wife had given him a list and some money and he'd hitched up the wagon-team and headed out early that morning, with good ole Petey underfoot all the way. He could make Waco, get the stuff and start back all in the same day. He'd be forced to camp along the way overnight on the return to the farm.

"What'll ya' have?" the bartender asked.

"Beer," Tobe Kirkwood said. "Gimme a beer."

He was not much of a drinking man, he knew it, and he had never even tasted whiskey, but he drank a beer every time he came into a town, mostly for the sociable part of it, talking to other men in the place, gathering intelligence. It made him feel light-headed, he had no intentions of drinking enough to get drunk and be a fool.

He listened to his companions at the bar talk and learned little They talked mostly of the weather and cattle and everyday stuff, a little politics. He had seen Union soldiers in town on his first trip for supplies, on this trip he had seen none so he felt no pressure.

They probably didn't know about the reward on his head down here.

"What kinda law ya' got in this town?" he asked the bartender.

"German fella named Stegner, used to be a Ranger. He don't allow no foolishness. Practices with them pistols all the time and he'll shoot ya' in a heartbeat."

Tobe digested this information, thoughtfully finishing the last of the beer.

"I wanna send a letter back home. Where do I go to get it writ?"

"You can't write?"

"Naw. Had my cousin's wife write a letter for me a couple o' months ago, but this time I don't want her knowin' my business."

"There's a man down the street, second door on the left, he writes letters for people."

"Thanks."

Tobe found the man and sent a second letter home to his mother in Tennessee. This one included the news that he might be moving, going to Mexico, he would write her again when he got the chance. There was no reason for the cousin or his wife to know he might be leaving. This way they would not know until he wanted them to know. He paid the man, signed his big X on the bottom and mailed the letter.

He looked longingly at the women in front of the cribs as he drove the wagon out of town. Maybe next time. He didn't have much money and none to waste on pleasure now, but soon he would consider it. He hadn't had a woman since the last time with that hateful Hattie. He despised her, but he missed her, and he missed the great Southern mountains he had left behind.

***

Marshal Stegner led the pair into his office and they sat on worn wooden chairs while he rummaged through his desk drawers, looking for something. Venus was nervous, her eyes darting everywhere, taking in the gun rack, the desks, the door to the jail section. Hattie was calmer, though on the inside she, too, was concerned.

"Here it is," he said finally, producing a letter from the desk. 'You wanna read it?"

Hattie took the letter and looked at it. On the outside of the envelope it was addressed in a straggly handwriting "City Police, Waco, Texas."

She opened the letter and began to read, quickly realizing it was from the doctor's wife they had tortured in Tennessee:

She is a fiend and a devil in women clothing who hurt me with a knife and threaten to do worse. I cannot tell horros this girl put on me, her and vile companions. Robbed me and cut me and like to have kill me. She is with two outlaw men and a nigger girl. I believe they may come to you town. Hold for officers, write me if you catch them...

"Are you going to put us in jail?" Hattie said, watching closely to see the marshal's reaction.

"No, not right now anyway," he said. *She was a handsome woman, maybe twenty years old* he thought, *full-figured, but not a cow like some of the women in his sporting house. She might be useful, also the colored girl.*

"What are you two doin' in Waco?"

"Looking for my cousin, he's supposed to be down here," Hattie lied.

"I've got a place you can work," Marshal Stegner said. "Come with me."

At the fancy house, Venus was put to work in the kitchen. Hattie was shown to a bedroom upstairs.

"The two of you can share this bedroom until you find a better place," he said. "It's awful noisy here, but you'll be able to sleep purty good during the week. I'll see you again tomorrow."

***

Hattie's eyes got wide as Jo explained the function of the house to her late that afternoon. She had heard of things like this, but never been near one. She and Venus met the rest of the women at supper, wher they all sat down around a big table in the kitchen and ate together.

"What's he got in mind for me, Jo?"

"Girl, he wants you fer hisself first. After that, he may put you to work here or over at the saloon."

"How 'bout Venus?"

"We don't work any colored girls here, so she'll have to stay in the kitchen."

"He said he'll see me tomorrow. When do you suppose that'll be?"

"When he comes here to be with one of the other girls, it's usually right after dinner. I'd say about one o'clock in the afternoon that's when he'll come to see you."

Hattie and Venus slept together in the big double bed in their room, giggling like school girls and talking into the night.

"What you gonna do, Hattie?"

"I don't know. Maybe I'll run."

"We kin get the hosses ready and ride outta here early in the mornin'."

"No, just let me think. I'll tell you tomorrow."

She tossed and turned and thoughts ran through her head. Sex with a stranger was not impossible, it depended on the payoff. She would not be turned into a common prostitute, to be sold to men. That was out of the question, but Granny's advice came back to mind. She was a woman, too weak to fight a man like Tobe Kirkwood head-on. Her weapons were her ability to think, to influence, to nag if need be. To get a man or a group of men to do her work. The Yankee patrol had failed, but maybe this cool, blue-eyed German lawman with the holstered pistols under his coat could do the job.

And she was confident in her body. She had been treated roughly by Kirkwood on occasion, but she had also been amused to see him flame with desire for her body, so hungry for her that he fumbled and hurried with his clothing, so anxious to get to her. She had almost laughed at his kissing of her breasts, as greedy as a child at the nipple, the red-headed beast of the mountains shuddering with lust for her.

If she could tame Tobe Kirkwood with her body, then she could also take in this city marshal. Later, he might be the very man to help her get Tobe. It was a purely business decision, she thought, you have to give something to get something.

***

The next morning she confided in Jo that she wanted something nice to wear, a nightgown to make her look her best for the marshal. Jo searched the bureau in her own room and came up with a lacy white thing

"Here, girl, wear this. You'll look like a bride on her wedding night, he'll love it."

"Let me see that."

"Y'ever been married, girl? Have any children?"

"Yeah, I was married back home," Hattie said, thinking of Tobe Kirkwood and the guerilla wedding. "I lost a baby, nearly killed me."

"Tha's all right, honey, " Jo said, mothering her suddenly, patting her shoulder. "I'm sorry y'r baby died."

"Where can I take a bath?"

"Get that darkie girl o' yours to heat up some water," Jo said. 'We got a big tub out here in the woodshed, you can take a bath there."

With Venus helping her, Hattie took a long, soaking bath in the woodshed, washing her hair and drying it in the sun. She ate dinner with the other women at noon and then went alone to her room to await the marshal.

He was right on time, depending on Jo and the others to have told the girl what was expected, what to do for him. She did not disappoint him.

He knocked gently on the door and she told him to come in. He came into the room, which was piled high with all the clothing and gear Hattie and Venus had brought on their trip, including even their saddles. Hattie's rifle stood in a corner, there were clothes both dirty and fresh-washed everywhere.

He took off his hat and looked once at her and from then on, all else was ignored, forgotten in the moment. Hattie June Rose, fresh from the wild Appalachian mountains, was breath-takingly beautiful in the transparent white gown Jo had given her. She had nothing on underneath and he could see the shape of her body, her dark nipples showing plainly through the lace.

"Like what you see, Marshal?" she taunted.

"Girl, I'm ready for you."

"I believe you are," she cooed, coming to him and rubbing his hardness with her hand. "Take some of these clothes off so we can get together."

She unbuckled his pistols and helped him take off his clothing and they soon lay nude on the tangled bed. He kissed her clumsily and she was pleased at his insistent desire for her.

In an instant, she rolled onto her back and he entered her, plunging and surging and making the rickety bed groan and rock with his efforts. Then release, and he was gone, driving deep inside her. It was that quick.

He had had dozens of women, but there was something about her that was different, an independence, a sassy air, confidence. Whatever it was, he soon stopped trying to figure it out, he liked it, and he was enjoying it.

Like a schoolboy with his first love, the marshal was infatuated with this newly-arrived mountain girl and he visited her again the next day and twice more before the week was out. From his manner, Jo knew that Hattie was not to be treated like a regular, not to be used in the trade, but was to be saved for the marshal. Hattie, of course, knew it from the beginning and the other girls soon sensed it.

"Hell, girl, he might even marry you," one said at breakfast.

"No," Hattie smiled. "I'm not ready to get married again. I got hurt bad losing that baby. I don't think I'll ever be able to have children again."

"He don't want kids, Hattie, he just wants you."

***

After sex, they lay in the big bed and he talked to her, about the Rangering days, about his businesses, he told her things he had never told anyone. She pondered his business deals and thought over things.

They soon settled into a routine and the marshal, whether he admitted it or not, was falling deeply in love. Hattie was not, but she liked the attention and was fond of the tall lawman, so passionate in the afternoons. She walked around town with him, sat and drank beer with him in his saloon and began to make suggestions, which were soon implemented.

"The sporting house is losing business to the cheap whores who work the cribs," she told Jo. "The marshal's got a rule against drinking that keeps things quiet here in the house, but we've got to loosen up a little bit and we'll get more business for it."

"What're ya' talkin' about, honey?"

"The marshal don't want the girls drinking with the customers, don't want whiskey even in the house, right?"

"Yeah, the customers we get just come in here and go right to the girls. We've always run it that way."

"Well, let's face it. Lots of men are scared of women, they need a drink before they can talk about what they really want."

So with the marshal's steady backing, Hattie had carpenters come and the big house was enlarged, adding two more rooms. A small bar was installed in a corner downstairs.

"Are we hiring a bartender?" the marshal asked.

"No, we'll use Venus. She can pour whiskey as good as anybody."

The marshal smoked cigars and Hattie noticed that, too. The drovers and teamsters and farmhands she saw around Waco were also fond of cigars, especially after a meal or when they were drinking.

"I want our customers to have a cigar when they leave," she announced. "I want to set it up so they pay one price to get a drink, a girl and a cigar.

"They pay at the front door and we'll give 'em something, maybe a button or something, to show that they paid in full. Then they get the drink first, then the girl and then the cigar when they leave."

Jo and the marshal liked the idea and a girl was sent out to a store to buy a whole box of red buttons. It worked well, even better than Hattie had planned.

Jo collected all the money at the front door, giving each man a shiny red button. This meant that the girls did not collect, or steal any of the money as they had done in the past. Venus tended bar, serving one honest drink of regular bar whiskey to each customer.

The men had only to show their red buttons to Venus and the girl for service. On their way out, they gave the buttons back to Jo, who gave each of them a good cigar, the same brand that the marshal smoked.

Satisfied men on the streets of Waco smoking cigars became walking advertisements for the house and its new operating policy was soon common knowledge.

"Look at that smoke," companions would crow when the lucky man returned to his fellows. "Been over at the big house, ain't ya'?" Business boomed and they were able to command a premium price and still keep all the girls busy. "Good service is worth a good price," Hattie told them.

At the saloon, Hattie watched Moody dealing cards and the bartenders who sold whiskey for them there. It was a good saloon, but it had only an ordinary trade and she wanted to improve it.

She found her answer in conversation one day with one of the girls who was working the saloon, rotated on duty from the big house, a new girl that Marshal Stegner had hired off the street. The girl had come from New Orleans, she said, and in conversation mentioned that she had also danced in a Louisiana music hall.

"You know how to dance?" Hattie asked.

"Sure, nothing to it. I might be a little rusty, but I used to dance in a line of girls every night. Gotta have music and I can do it good as any."

They bought a piano from a defunct church and

put up a sign out front "Piano Player Wanted." In a week they had a player, also from Louisiana, who had played (he said) in some of the better sporting houses and would work for drinks and tips.

At Hattie's urging, the dancing whore taught two others how to hoof and they had 'shows' which consisted of the girls dancing to the piano music. Their musician commented that their shows were tame compared to those in New Orleans, but they were racy for Waco and the saloon was soon crowded every night.

Moody added another dealer and then a third, to take care of the gambling interests and the marshal's businesses boomed, thanks to his new woman.

She was sitting with the marshal in the saloon, at a corner table where they could watch the festivities, when word came that Ben Callahan was on a rip in a bad whiskey-joint three blocks away.

"He's always been bad to fight when he's a-drinkin', Marshal," the messenger said, "but this time he's killed a man, the fella's lyin right there dead, stabbed in th' heart, sittin' thar in a chair, right in the middle of the place. Got his pistol layin' on the table, right in front of' im. An' he's good with it."

"Anybody else in there with Ben?"

"Naw, nobody 'cept the bartender. He had to stay, and besides, he's keepin 'im supplied with whiskey. Ben says he's gonna kill you, Marshal, when ya' come to get him."

"Yeah, he said that last time," the marshal said drily. "I locked him up and the judge finally come around and gave him a fine and turned him loose."

The messenger dodged back out into the night and Hattie touched the marshal's arm, concern in her eyes.

"Don't go by yourself, Marshal," she said. "Get some deputies to help you."

"I can handle this one," he said. "It won't take long."

"Wait a minute, what if there's another man or two hiding there? What if this is an ambush?"

"You're too suspicious, Hattie. I've heard some of your tales about bushwhacking in the mountains, but this ain't that kind of a deal. It's just what it seems to be, a drunk with a pistol and a knife holed up in a whiskey-joint, roughest place in this town."

"So what are you planning to do?"

"Well, I'll tell you. This place he's at started out as a tent, then th' next owner managed to nail up a shack made out of old lumber an' tha's all it is now. Cheapest rotgut whiskey you can buy, dirt floor covered with sawdust, th' bar is just some planks laid across sawhorses, it's nothin' but a hole. And I'm shore thankful it's got two doors, one in the front and one in the back. I'll be going in the back."

"And I'll be going in the front," Hattie said triumphantly, amazed at her own ideas. "I'll walk right in the front and while he's looking at me, you can slip in the back and catch him."

"Naw," the marshal protested. "I don't need a woman to help me do my work."

"I'll tell you more about my bushwhacking days tomorrow," she said firmly. "I've probably seen more killing than you have, don't worry about me." She patted her purse then and he knew what the lump in it was, he'd seen her shoot the cap-and-ball .36 a time or two during his practice sessions at the vacant lot. She was a fair shot, especially at close ranges.

He knew there was no time, or reason, to argue with her. Her mind was made up and it was truly a good plan. With Ben Callahan's attention diverted, he would be an easy mark for the iron marshal, who did not intend to arrest him this time.

They walked the distance to the whiskey-shack and he showed her the front door. "Give me two minutes, no more, to get around back and then you come in the front door," he whispered, and was gone in the darkness.

She could see the interior of the place lit by oil lamps, a man at a table and another man behind the bar. The front windows were filthy, but she could make out the scene inside. When two minutes had gone, as best as she could judge in the darkness, Hattie pushed the rude door open and made her entrance.

The gunman at the table was surprised, his mouth dropped open.

His hand was on the pistol which lay on the table in front of him and she smiled and nodded at him as she walked to the bar. *He was maybe twenty feet from her,* she thought, *close enough to hit with the gun hidden in her purse if it came to that.*

"What do you want, lady?" the barkeeper growled. "You don't need to be in here."

"I want to buy a drink," Hattie said, staring down at the corpse on the floor. The dead man was lying face-down in the sawdust, one lifeless hand clutched to his chest, his hat lying beside him, near the table where the killer sat.

"You sell whiskey, don't you?" she asked politely. "Sell me a glass."

"Who are you?" yelled the gunman. "What in hell are you doin'? Get outta here, we don't need no women tonight."

"Come over here and talk to me," Hattie said sweetly. "I'm new in town and I don't know anybody around here."

His red eyes, filled with rage and whiskey, were locked on hers, but behind him she saw a dim form and movement.

"I said fer you to get outta here," Ben Callahan roared at Hattie, starting to rise to his feet to enforce the order. He never made it. He was aware of the marshal appearing at his immediate right, but it was too late.

The marshal had his Navy Colts in each hand, the hammers already eared back to full cock, and the sawdust had muffled his steps, and Ben Callahan's attention was on the dark-haired girl. When Ben tried to swing to his right, the marshal's hands began to manipulate the lethal Navies with deadly effect.

Both revolvers bucked and jumped in his hands as they speared red flame in the dimly-lit saloon, the heavy lead slugs slamming into the man's upper torso. His ex-Ranger instincts taking over, the marshal pumped six bullets into his opponent and they all found their mark. Ben Callahan toppled over, breaking the table in his fall, and was dead by the time he hit the floor beside his victim.

Hattie looked at the two dead men on the floor and the marshal standing there grinning, the smoking Colts in his hands. "All of a sudden I'm not thirsty," she told the bartender. "You better drink that one yourself, you work in a bad place."

They walked out of the gunsmoke that night and grew even closer. Marshal Stegner was head-over-heels in love with the Southern girl and he knew it, but did not know yet what to do about it. He only knew that he wanted to be with her all the time, he enjoyed their romps in the bed in the afternoon immensely. "I just cain't get enough of you, Hattie," he'd whisper when it was over.

But he loved her mind, too, the way she could figure things out. Her common sense, her practical approach to situations, he loved her more than any woman he'd ever had.

Hattie, however, was still on the track of a murderer and the thoughts filled her mind constantly. She liked the marshal, she was fond of him and his gentle strength, but she had no plans for the future, no dreams beyond her favorite dream of seeing Big Tobe Kirkwood dead.

Now she told it all.

"I was what you would call the common-law wife of the biggest Rebel bushwhacker in the mountains," she told the marshal, and she was gratified to see that his manner toward her did not change. She saw no jealousy or anger in him toward her. He listened quietly, asking a question here and there in the manner of a practiced lawman who had interrogated many prisoners.

"I did the thinking and the planning and helped with the work, and me and Tobe Kirkwood killed a slew of Yankees," she told him. "My own Daddy got killed by Unions and Tobe helped me get the very men that did it. I shot two of them myself, with the pistol I keep with me now.

"Tobe, the hateful bastard, killed my own little brother, after I told him not to. That's why we're here, me and Venus, to get Tobe. Not to find my cousin, like I told you at first. Here, look at this."

She produced the tintype photo then from her purse and, for the first time, brought out the gold watch

Kirkwood had taken from the dead Payne at Copperhill. The Masonic emblem still hung from the gold chain.

"Lemme see that," the marshal said, curiously looking at the timepiece and the chain. "I'm a Mason myself, belong to the lodge here in town. This bushwhacker killed a Mason?"

"Sure. Killed dozens of people. At one time had fifty men that rode with him, claimed he was my husband. They called him the red-headed butcher of the mountains."

She told him about the failed attempt to bushwhack Tobe then, sparing no details. She even told about the baby inside her and how she felt so bad when Tobe Kirkwood rode off loose and unhurt, that she tried to hang herself and lost the baby.

The marshal impulsively hugged her, cuddling this girl who had lost so much; so innocent and yet so hard, focused on her mission. He wanted to protect her, to keep her safe from harm, yet he knew she was perfectly capable of protecting herself if it came down to that. He held her close and chuckled deep in his chest, he was hopelessly in love with her and he knew it, completely under her influence.

"There is one other thing that might help," she said. "We got the old woman in Tennessee to tell us. He's working on his cousin's farm out here somewhere, supposed to be fairly close to Waco. The cousin's name is Samuels, that's the last name, don't know the first name."

"Lots of new folks coming in to Texas all the time," he told her, "never heard of this Samuels. The farm could be twenty, thirty miles from here and they may not come into town very often, but surely we can find 'em, let me have that picture for a day or two."

She gave him the watch, too and he put it in his desk, sometimes taking it out to look at it and stare at the Masonic symbol. The fact that this man had killed a Mason made it personal for him, he took a strong interest in the case now.

The tintype was handled and looked at by the women who worked in the cribs first. They met a lot of men, but a red-headed man was fairly rare, they said, and they did not recognize Tobe Kirkwood.

The marshal showed it to bartenders in the cheap whiskey joints as well as his own saloon. And the barkeep in the joint where Tobe had lingered over his beer remembered the man.

"Can't tell you much about him, Marshal," he said. "He asked some questions and went down the street. I think he paid a feller to write letters home for him."

The letter-writer was not much help, but gave a little more information on Tobe Kirkwood. In conversation, while the letter was being done, he had volunteered that he was working on a farm about a day's ride from Waco and he got supplies at a certain store.

At the store, the people remembered Tobe, who had paid with cash money. They seemed to think the farm he hauled supplies to was located west of Waco. Yes, they said, he came into town about once a month.

***

The fancy house sat on a large, full lot which extended from one street to another. It had a small front yard, but a large yard in the back, which accommodated the woodshed, the privy and a big clothesline. A picket fence with a gate surrounded the back yard area.

The whores used a lot of clothing and Hattie insisted that the sheets on the beds be changed regularly. Venus and the kitchen help had to hustle to do the laundry three times a week and keep the food coming, too. Hattie helped with the laundry sometimes, especially when some of her own clothing was being washed, she wanted it done right.

"She's bossy as hell, ain't she?" the working girls complained, for Hattie had simply laid down a rule that one of the whores had to help with the laundry, too, each time it was done. The duty was a rotating one, so only one whore would be working with the kitchen crew on laundry each time.

Today it was a fat girl from Arkansas named Tootsie, who didn't complain much and actually liked the break in her routine, helping Venus and Hattie and the two cooks.

The cooks were boiling water in a big washpot over a smoky fire, with Tootsie and Venus scrubbing the clothes on a washboard, up to their elbows in the soapy hot water.

Hattie was hanging the fresh-washed clothes on the line, her hair pinned up to keep it out of her face. Somewhere in her subconscious, she must have heard the wagon coming down the dirt street by the yard-fence, but she did not notice it.

When she heard a dog growling at the gate, Hattie glanced and her heart stopped. It was a red bulldog, an animal that had never liked her, it was Petey.

Her hands frozen on the clothesline, she lifted her eyes to stare at the wagoneer and met the steady, hateful gaze of Big Tobe Kirkwood.

Chapter Thirteen

"Hattie, you goddamn little bitch," Tobe roared, standing in the wagon and bringing the Spencer up to his shoulder.

She turned to run and he fired immediately, the bullet clipping the clothesline which parted and dropped the heavy wet wash to the ground. Tootsie screamed in terror at the washboard and Petey began to howl and bite viciously at the picket-fence gate, trying to get in.

Lifting her dress high with both hands, Hattie ran at full speed toward the back door of the house and Tobe shot at her again, the rifle blast deafening at close range, the bullet kicking up dirt beside her churning legs, but missing.

"God-amighty, he's gonna kill 'er," Tootsie shrieked. "Oh Lord, run."

Venus scooted into the woodshed and came out with her pistol blazing, shooting at Tobe at an angle across the fence. From where she was standing, she was facing his team, but she could see him plainly standing in the wagon, his rifle leveled at the fleeing Hattie.

Her first shot, aimed at Tobe, went low and killed one of his wagon horses, striking the animal between the eyes. It fell kicking and thrashing, the other horse now snorting and rearing in fear. The struggling of the surviving horse brought the wagon forward with a lurch and Tobe fired at Hattie the third time just as it happened, his shot thrown well off the mark.

She had reached the back door of the house now and the slug missed her a good ten feet, shattering a window in the kitchen as she plunged through the door to safety. Aware of the shooting aimed at him Tobe turned to face Venus and levered the deadly Spencer to kill her.

Venus thumbed back the hammer on her pistol for another shot and aimed right at Tobe. When the gun kicked in her hand, his hat flew off and he shot the rifle at her. She felt a tremendous blow to her head and fell to the ground.

Bare-headed and slightly dazed by the fast action, Tobe Kirkwood looked around the battle scene for a moment and fled, the bulldog trailing him. Hattie was gone, the colored girl was lying lifeless in the yard and one of his team was obviously dead in the harness. Rifle in hand, he ran down the street and quickly vanished.

Hattie dashed upstairs and returned to the fray with her own pistol in hand, but Tobe was gone, and Venus was down. Down but still breathing, it turned out, the pulse beating strongly under Hattie's probing fingers. Gawking bystanders were gathering now, wandering around the wagon and peering over the fence at the colored girl lying on the ground.

"You got a knife?" Hattie asked one of the men. He looked wide-eyed at the gun in her hand and nodded.

"Then cut the dead horse loose from the harness," she ordered, "and you other men get over here and help me load this girl on the wagon."

In a minute or two, they had hacked away the heavy harness leather from the dead horse and loaded Venus in the back of the wagon. Her pistol still in hand, Hattie climbed onto the wagon seat and whipped the remaining horse into action, the scraps of harness from the dead horse dragging in the dust.

The frantic run down the streets of Waco soon brought the wagon into Tobe's view, where he stood in the shadows of a building. He followed from a distance, the two-horse wagon now pulled by only one animal being conspicuous among the other teams on the streets.

Hattie drove fast and soon had more volunteers bearing the limp Venus up the steps to the doctor's second-floor office above a hardware store. Word had reached the marshal and he came to her there.

Tobe watched from the shadows and saw the marshal and a deputy climbing the steps to the doctor's office. He saw no reason for a showdown now and melted away into the alleys and back streets, where he soon stole a horse and rode quietly out of town.

"Come on, Petey," he said. "We'll go camp down on the river for a few days. Come back when everything's quietened down and fix Hattie fer good."

Five miles down the Brazos, they found an old man camping alone and made a friendly arrangement with him, staying there in the brush. The old man liked Petey immediately and scratched the bulldog's head, which Petey liked.

***

At the doctor's office, Venus was treated by the physician and by late afternoon she was sitting up, but very groggy. He got the bleeding stopped and wrapped her head in a white gauze bandage.

"She's gonna have a hell of a headache," the doctor told Hattie and the marshal, "but she's young and strong and the bullet just barely grazed her skull. Take her home."

They half-dragged, half-carried the weak Venus to the wagon and got her back to their room and into the bed. She ate a little, fed by one of the cooks, and soon dropped into a deep sleep. Hattie left her then and went with the marshal to the saloon.

"He's stole a horse, the deputies found that out," the marshal said. "He's gone. You might see him come back or he may never pass through here again."

"He stole a horse 'cause he's too lazy to walk," Hattie snapped. "That don't bother him at all. He's just come out of a war where he stole horses all the time, we all stole horses if we needed them."

"Well, don't steal none around here," the marshal said lamely. There was a lot about this fiery Southern girl he did not know and talk of horse-stealing went against his grain. The marshal was a very moral man.

"He'll come back," Hattie said. "You can count on that. Maybe tonight, maybe tomorrow, but real soon, and he'll kill anybody that gets in his way. Cause he wants to kill me, real bad."

"You people hold a grudge the worst I ever saw," the marshal said. "We're just regl'r Americans around here. Some people don't like Mexicans or Indians, but they don't hate 'em all personally. They wouldn't ride halfway across the whole country just to shoot one. Y'all are different."

"We are not," Hattie hissed at him, her eyes glancing sparks. 'We're just as American as anybody else. It's just this terrible bad blood between me and Tobe," she said, calming down some. "It ain't gonna end til one of us is dead, maybe both of us. I've already told you all about it."

"You sleep tonight in one of the rooms here," the marshal said, gesturing up the wooden stairs. "In case he comes to the house looking for you. The bartenders always keep shotguns behind the bar and me and the deputies can guard you better here."

***

The next morning at breakfast, she told him of her plan. She had thought of it that morning, when her mind was fresh and her ideas came better.

"Give me that tintype back," she asked and he did, producing the metal photo from his vest pocket. "I'm going to a printer this morning and set some traps for ol' Tobe."

The printer had a helper who was a fair artist and he set the little picture of Tobe on a board in front of him while he worked. Hattie told him of the red hair and beard, and of the ear half-shot away by Yankee bullets. He drew, and re-drew, until she was satisfied.

"We'll print 'em this afternoon, let 'em dry overnight," the printer said. "You can pick 'em up tomorrow morning, ma'am, and we thank you for the business."

The marshal looked over the posters when she brought them to his office the next morning. It was a good likeness of Tobe Kirkwood, he guessed, judging from the tintype. Hattie had made the artist draw it on a slightly different angle, showing plainly the half-ear.

"That's a lot o' money, Hattie, that'll get every man in town after yore old boyfriend, or husband, or whatever he is."

"That's the idea," Hattie said, smiling at her handiwork. "A woman's got to be smarter'n a man cause she's not as strong or as fast."

"I kinda feel sorry for the ol' boy myself."

"Well, I don't. I'd like to shoot him myself, but this way I've got lots of help. And this is the way I want to do it," she said. "Have the deputies to hand 'em out, but I don't want any of these posted. You understand?"

He understood and he and the deputies took the posters around.

"I want every storekeeper and every bartender and every whore and gambler in town to have one of these. I had plenty printed up," Hattie told them. "But not a one is to be posted, cause I don't want Tobe to know. Tell 'em to keep the posters hidden away, and to send word as soon as he shows up."

The posters were given out, every one, with a good likeness of the wanted man and the $5,000 REWARD heading. At the bottom of the poster it said to contact Commanding Officer, U.S. Army, Cleveland, Tennessee, to claim the money.

**

Five days later, Tobe and Petey slipped back into town. He was tired of eating fish and camping on the river with the old man and he was ready to deal with Hattie June Rose.

"C'mon, Petey," he said gruffly. "It's payback time. We're gonna find Hattie."

On the stolen horse, he rode slowly into Waco and tied it in an alley, beside a big dry-goods store. Then he quietly walked around back and entered a cheap saloon through its rear door. He was seen and recognized immediately and a messenger sent to find the marshal, but Tobe went unsuspecting to the bar, got a beer and took it with him to a table where he could watch the door. His plan was simple, he would drink the beer and then go to the house where he had last seen Hattie and kill her. They would not be expecting him in broad daylight.

The bartender recognized him, too, but wanted the reward and very quickly had a plan of his own. He had the reward poster on a shelf behind the bar and the red hair and half-ear were easy to spot. Greedy for the money, he motioned to two drifters to come to the bar and whispered his plan to them. They were the only other men in the place. Tobe sat at his table in the shadows across the room, the Spencer across his knees and sipped his beer, watching them.

Then the bartender was walking across the room toward him, carrying a foaming mug of beer in his hand, the two drifters coming along behind him.

"Here's ya' some more beer, mister," the bartender said. "It's free, on the house." Petey sat up now, alert to the approaching men, and growled.

"I didn't order no beer," Tobe said, his hands dropping to the repeating rifle in his lap.

The bartender threw the beer at Tobe then, but his aim was too high and it clattered off the wall behind Tobe. He reached into his front pants pocket, under a greasy apron, and produced a small pistol, but Tobe had kicked the table into the midst of the approaching trio and, as they dodged it, he let the Spencer talk, shooting from the hip at point-blank range.

He fired again and again and again, working the lever and hosing down the three men with heavy rifle-slugs. The bartender fell first, hit twice through the chest and then the nearer drifter. Oblivious to the gun, Petey dived into the melee and bit the other drifter in the leg. The man squalled like a river panther and ran for the front door, dragging Petey behind him. Tobe tried one shot at the runner and he staggered, hit in the shoulder, but managed to break free from the dog and vanished into the street.

Gunsmoke filled the barroom, in layers in the sunlight, and Tobe stepped over his two victims and walked behind the bar. There he saw the clean white poster and picked it up. He could not read his name, but he certainly recognized his own face.

Damn you, Hattie, he thought, *you done this to me. Setting me up again fer ambush, just like ya done with them Yankee soldiers. I gotta get.*

He picked up the pistols from the dead bartender and drifter.

Neither had gotten off a shot, their guns were still fully loaded. He stuck the handguns in his belt and, with Petey, headed back out the rear door.

The thunder of gunfire early in the morning inside the saloon was heard by the whole neighborhood. The marshal and his deputies were running, just two blocks away, when the last echoes of the Spencer died away.

Tobe and Petey ran into the alley and he mounted the horse, but it was too late. Lawmen and armed citizens sealed both ends of the alley. Tobe drew the pistols from his belt and kicked the horse, he could still charge through them to escape. He managed only two or three wild shots before it was all over.

Experienced manstoppers, the marshal's deputies both had rifles and simply shot the horse down first, aiming for the heart and lungs, as they would on a deer. The animal plunged and reared once, then toppled over forward.

Thrown from the saddle, Tobe hit the ground unharmed, but took nearly a dozen bullets trying to regain his feet. The Waco marshal, they said afterwards, walked in on him with both Navies blazing and just never missed. Tobe was hit in both legs and several times through the abdomen and chest. They kicked his pistols away and he lay in the dirt looking up at them, coughing up blood and slowly dying.

"Ya' killed my hoss and my dog, too," he said. The marshal nodded. One of the civilians had thoughtfully shot the vicious dog with a shotgun and Petey was quite dead, lying against a rain-barrel at the corner of the alley entrance.

Hattie arrived and walked into the scene, lifting her skirts high to keep out of the dirt and blood of the alley. She stared down at Tobe, smeared with blood and gore, but still faintly alive.

"Hello, Hattie, my good little wife," he taunted. "You bein' good out here in Texas?"

"I'm not your damn wife, Tobe," she said through gritted teeth. "The only thing I hate about this is that I didn't get to kill you myself."

"Looks like these other fellas beat ya' to it, girl. I'm hurtin' bad, I'm a-dyin' fer sure."

"And I'm glad of it," she said. "You didn't need to kill Little Buck. Hurry up and die, I hope you rot in hell."

Big Tobe Kirkwood never spoke again after that exchange and his eyes rolled back in his head and his chest stopped moving. The guerilla chief was finally dead, killed by a Texas peace officer.

***

They had called a photographer that day and the little man had come into the bloody alley and photographed everything there. At Hattie's insistence, they had propped up the dead outlaw against the wall of the store and took several pictures of him. She also demanded that the photographer take close-up pictures showing his face and the mutilated ear, for proof of identity.

Then they had put him in a plain wooden box and Hattie had put a scrap of blood-stiffened cloth in the box with him, the piece of Little Buck's death-shirt she had carried so far and so long. The box they buried in Boot Hill.

***

Hattie did it up right. Letters and affidavits from witnesses, plus the photographs of the dead Tobe, were sent to the Union Army in Cleveland, Tennessee. Also, just for good measure, she sent letters to the Cleveland newspaper and to the doctor's wife, to let the family know where he was buried.

A great sense of relief filled Hattie in the days after Tobe was slain and she soon began to feel restless. The marshal could sense it and knew he might be losing her.

"God, Hattie, don't go away. I love you, girl."

"I know," she said gently, kissing his lips. "I know, and you've been so good to me, but I'm not ready to settle down yet."

"I can make you happy here, give you anything you want, you know that."

She shook her head and bit her lip, trying to put it into words he could understand. "Gus, the War was not over for me til I got Tobe. That's the way it was, I was still fightin' the War. Now it's done, finally done.

"But I can't go home like these soldiers you see coming back now. I did what I had to do, but half my county back home hates me for it. My daddy and my brother both got killed and they'd get me, too, if I go back. I want to see California. Maybe I'll come back here in a year or two."

Moody gave her the names of some gamblers he knew in San Francisco, and neither Moody nor the marshal complained when she took a large wad of money from the saloon and the sporting house. With it she outfitted herself and Venus for the trip.

They were both wearing fine dresses and hats with feathers in them, on matching saddle-horses and proper side-saddles, when they rode out. Hattie had hired a Mexican boy about twelve years old to go with them. He rode a burro and led their pack mule, he would look after the stock and build the cooking fire each night.

Marshal August Stegner stood in a daze on the main dusty street of Waco and watched in silence as they rode away that last morning.

She had promised to write him, but she never did.

And he never forgot her.

THE END

Meet our Author

Wally Avett

Wally Avett is retired from a sales career: newspaper and billboard advertising, mobile homes, real estate- in the Great Smoky Mountains of North Carolina. He lives in the same little town, sometimes compared to Mayberry, where he was editor of the weekly newspaper in the '70's and town manager in the '80's.

"My father was a town-and-country Methodist preacher," he says. "So I grew up with good story-telling all around me, friends and family." He met many colorful characters in a lifetime of interviews, heard many stories and they inspire his writing today.

"For me, good writing has to be based on truth. It gives the work an authentic ring and makes it believable. So I write like a granny-woman makes a quilt, producing fiction actually imagined from bits and pieces of raw truth."

He is an avid reader and a gardener, a Sunday School teacher and gospel singer, hunter, fisherman and reluctant handyman. He likes local history, sometimes sells cabins to Florida flatlanders and frequently tells funny stories.

His first two novels were published by Belle Books in 2014, *MURDER IN CANEY FORK* and *LAST BIGFOOT IN DIXIE*.

Made in the USA
Columbia, SC
19 August 2018